ZONDERKIDZ

Chosen Ones
Copyright © 2010 by Alister McGrath
Illustrations © 2010 by Wojciech Voytek Nowakowski

This title is also available as a Zondervan ebook.
Visit www.zondervan.com/ebooks.

Requests for information should be addressed to:

Zonderkidz, *Grand Rapids, Michigan* 49530

This edition: ISBN 978-0-310-72192-5 (softcover)

Library of Congress Cataloging-in-Publication Data

McGrath, Alister E., 1953–
    Chosen ones / Alister E. McGrath.
        p. cm. – (The Aedyn chronicles ; bk. 1)
        Summary: When Peter and Julia go to stay with their grandparents in Oxford,
England, they discover a mysterious garden, which serves as a portal to a world
where they are greeted as the saviors of a people enslaved by evildoers.
        ISBN 978-0-310-71812-3 (hardcover)
        [1. Fantasy. 2. Brothers and sisters – Fiction. 3. Good and evil – Fiction.] I.
Title.
    PZ7.M169477Ch 2010
    [Fic] – dc22   2009044776

Published in association with the literary agency of Alive Communications, Inc.,
7680 Goddard Street, Suite 200, Colorado Springs, CO 80920,
www.alivecommunications.com.

Zonderkidz is a trademark of Zondervan.

Editor: Kathleen Kerr
Art direction: Cindy Davis
Cover design: Sarah Molegraaf
Interior design & composition: Luke Daab & Carlos Eluterio Estrada

Printed in the United States of America

11 12 13 14 15 16 /DCI/ 22 21 20 19 18 17 16 15 14 13 12 11 10 9 8 7 6 5 4 3 2 1

THE AEDYN CHRONICLES

BOOK ONE

CHOSEN ONES

Alister McGrath

ZONDERVAN.com/
AUTHORTRACKER
follow your favorite authors

Prologue

Ten little ships raced across the sea, seeking safety from the disaster that engulfed their island. Men, women, children, and animals looked back in fear. Beyond the foamy wake of their ships they could see a plume of smoke and ash rising into the sky, spreading out against the horizon as it hit the atmosphere. The flashes of light and sheets of flame illum inated the ash. Some of the passengers wept, reduced to tears at the sight of their homeland's devastation.

Those in the first ship looked anxiously towards their leader. Marcus could save them, if anyone could. He had warned them of a coming disaster, had urged them to flee. He had supervised the building of ships and the loading of provisions for a voyage. Yet nobody really knew where they were bound—if they had any destination beyond a watery grave. None of the great sages had ever spoken of land beyond the southern horizon. Yet that was the course Marcus had set for them.

Days passed without any sign of land. Marcus kept watch at the bow, peering into the emptiness, trying to conceal his growing anxiety from those around him. Somewhere ahead there had to be an island—an island that appeared on no maps. Above him the eagles circled, searching for signs of land. Yet nothing had yet been seen. Marcus wondered, not for the first time, if he had been mistaken. But he squared his shoulders and kept his hardened eyes on the horizon. Everything depended on him.

CHAPTER

1

Once upon a time an old house stood in the English town of Oxford. It was built close by the ancient city walls, ivy growing over its stonework and mullioned windows, and was the sort of place with lots of dark corners and hidden stairways. And in this house lived a professor, his wife, and an old tabby cat.

The professor's special interest was reading about ancient battles, both at land and at sea. His ramshackle study was filled with paintings of famous naval engagements. The professor had never actually been to sea but rather liked the idea of it, and no one was prouder when his son became a captain in the Royal British Navy. His wife was the cozy, grandmotherly sort of person who specializes in scrumptious teas and biscuits. She had jolly round cheeks and an enormous lap for children to fall into.

On one particular day, not all that long ago, the house was all in a flurry of preparation for the arrival of two special visitors: their grandchildren. Their mother had died not quite a year ago, and with their father off at sea they needed a place to spend the school holidays. The professor's wife had spent the morning in preparation, airing out sheets and blankets, sweeping floors, and dusting cabinets. The professor had spent the morning choosing interesting books to leave in the spare bedrooms. For Peter, aged fourteen, he had selected a history of Admiral Nelson's tactics at the Battle of Trafalgar. It had been a bit more difficult for him to find a suitable book for Julia, aged thirteen, but finally he chose a fine book on ancient Greek politics and left it on her bedside table. His wife saw it as she placed a vase of freshly cut flowers from the garden by Julia's bed and hastily replaced it with a copy of *Alice in Wonderland*.

The children arrived that evening with all the ordinary bustle that completes a long journey. They were both hugged and kissed nearly to death, relieved of their bags, offered a vast assortment of sweet things, and shown to their rooms. Peter collapsed at once on top of his bed, not even bothering to undress, but Julia wasn't tired. She washed, changed into a long nightgown and sat on the edge of the bed, brushing her long hair absentmindedly and looking out through her window at a walled garden beneath her. She sighed deeply.

Normally, it had been agreed, she and Peter would be allowed to stay with friends during school breaks when their father was away. But this time their father had shore leave and was coming home to see them. There was something he had to tell them, he'd said in his message. So Julia and Peter had been told to go straight from their boarding schools to the old house in Oxford. Their father would join them there as soon as his ship docked in Plymouth.

Julia would have so much preferred to go to Lucy Honeybourne's home in Kent. They could have gone swimming together, and maybe even gone shopping in London for a day. She did love her grandparents, but they were so … well, so old-fashioned. Thank goodness they had finally left her alone for the night. She laid down the brush and leaned back on the pillow, riffling idly through the pages of *Alice in Wonderland* and listening to her brother's snores through the wall.

Julia did not really like Peter very much. He was interested in things that bored her, like machines and gadgets and sport, and since they had both been sent off to school they hardly ever saw each other. But, she admitted to herself, even Peter would be better company than her grandparents.

The thought froze in her head as her eyes and ears fixed themselves on the old ornate door. It was opening, slowly, creaking as a beam of light marched across the floor. But a moment later she relaxed. The old tabby cat had entered her room and leapt onto the bed beside her.

"Why, hello Scamp!" She lifted him up and tickled him under his chin. Scamp purred appreciatively. Both were glad to have some company. Julia walked to the window, scratching the tabby behind his ears as she went, and looked through the glass at the walled garden below, its fountain burbling gently.

"Look at that garden!" Scamp pressed a paw up against the cold pane and purred again. "Wouldn't you like to explore it! But you can't, because you're an inside cat. Aren't you?"

Scamp was not allowed outside the house in case he returned with fleas or freshly-killed birds or mice. Julia's grandmother was horrified at the thought of any of these creatures, living or dead, getting inside her nice clean house. She also did not want Scamp mixing with any of the rough, common cats that lived outside. He might learn some bad habits.

Julia gave a wry smile. Poor Scamp, always trapped inside! Suddenly, something moved in the garden below. Some birds were fluttering around the fountain. Scamp instantly became alert, his muscles tensed, staring down into the garden at the birds. Julia noticed his interest in what lay below. "You'd like to get out there and have an adventure, wouldn't you? Well, I'm sorry, but you aren't allowed out. You'll just have to stay here."

Julia dumped the old cat on her bed and watched him curl up into a ball and fall asleep. Making sure that Scamp did not follow her, she slid her feet into her blue slippers and descended the wooden staircase leading into the paneled hall. She wasn't tired—she was going to explore.

The house was still and quiet, apart from the slow ticking of an old grandfather clock. It was the first

time that Julia had ever been alone in the old house. She
began to investigate, peeping into rooms that she was
sure she was not meant to enter. She peeked into her
grandfather's study. What a mess! Papers were lying all
over the floor and books were stacked high on his desk.
There seemed to be a model of a sailing ship on every
shelf in the room. She shut the door quietly behind her
and moved on to the drawing room. After half an hour
she had explored every room in the house. What now?
Still wide awake, she loathed the idea of returning to the
stuffy spare room.

She was back in the hall. She ran her fingers along
its ancient wooden panels. To her left was the front door
leading towards the college. She had come through
that door earlier when she had arrived. But there was
another door to her right, half-hidden by a heavy green
curtain. She walked towards it and pushed the curtain
aside. Did it lead down to a cellar? Or out onto the street?
Making sure that Scamp was nowhere close, Julia slowly
unlocked the door and began to open it. The heavy oak
door creaked and groaned with the complaints of long
disuse, and Julia froze. What if someone heard and came
to investigate? Julia held her breath for a long moment,
but there was only silence.

Taking a deep breath, she opened the door completely to reveal a walled garden. It must be the same
garden that she could see from her bedroom. Julia

hesitated. Should she go in? She looked around quickly. Nobody was there! She entered the garden, closing the door as softly as she could behind her.

It was a glorious evening in the month of May. Silver light flashed off the streams of water from the fountain in its center. The soft burbling of the fountain echoed off the walls, enfolding the garden in its gentle music. At the side of the fountain was a small pond fed by its own stream of water. The walls were covered by trees and climbing plants. Apple trees, wisteria, and magnolia were all in bloom, the night air heavy with their fragrance. It was the most beautiful garden Julia had ever seen.

And then she heard a voice whisper her name, softly and slowly. A shiver shot down Julia's spine as she whipped around, looking for the source of the voice, but there was no one there. "Stop being stupid," she told herself, and gave a determined shake of her head before hurrying back inside the house. It must have been the wind, or birds, or someone talking in the street beyond the garden walls.

Julia closed the door softly behind her and returned to her room upstairs. Scamp was still curled up on the bed, and he stretched and flexed his claws as she turned back the covers and climbed in. It was an odd garden, she thought. Something wasn't right there.

And yet it looked so beautiful outside her window now, glowing softly. Silvery trees, silvery paths, silvery water. The fountain and pool were shimmering in an eerie yet beautiful light. There was something odd about it, she thought to herself. But she couldn't quite work out what it was.

Julia snuggled down beneath the covers, resolving to visit the garden again the next day. It was just as she finally fell asleep that she realized what was so strange about the garden. There had not been any moon that night.

She woke the next morning to a pressure on her shoulder and opened her eyes to see Scamp kneading his paws against her. Julia grinned sleepily and tickled his ears. The tabby leapt off the bed and meowed at the door.

"Ready for breakfast?" Julia asked her insistent companion. "I wouldn't mind a bit myself."

Her grandmother was already at the table downstairs, sipping a cup of tea as she perused the morning mail. She smiled as Julia appeared and gestured at the seat next to her. "Good morning, my dear," she murmured. "And where is that rascal brother of yours this morning?"

Her question was answered by a grunt. Peter loped into the room, still in yesterday's clothes, and plunked himself into a seat. It was, Julia decided, going to be a very long holiday.

Breakfast was a tense affair. The children's grandmother tried to get Peter and Julia to talk about their schools and their hobbies but, exhausting her arsenal of questions, she left the table and retreated into her quiet world of books and crochet. Peter asked permission to leave the house and explore Oxford, and Julia, delighted to be left in peace, took a book out to the garden that she had already begun to consider hers.

CHAPTER

2

The days fell into an easy routine. Peter would wake late in the mornings and head out to town in time for lunch with the professor. They spent their afternoons discussing Nelson's naval tactics and the development of gunpowder—"Boys' talk," according to Julia. She spent her time in the garden, reading or drawing or lying on her back doing absolutely nothing at all.

It was in such a mood one evening that she saw the glowing begin. She had, truth be told, almost entirely forgotten the silvery light that first evening in the garden, but now, watching the sun set over the garden walls, the strangeness of it could not be missed. There was a shimmer in the breeze and a sound like bells, but perhaps it was only in her mind. Julia sat up and looked around and gasped.

Every tree, every rock, every blade of grass seemed encased in a silver light all its own. The glow was stronger than it had been that other night, Julia thought—everything was sharper, clearer. She stood and moved around the garden, watching, drinking in the splendid light. She came to the edge of the pond and stopped, feeling a pull she could not quite define. Something was propelling her forward—something strong. Something powerful.

Another ringing—louder this time—brought her sharply out of the moment. Grandmother's dinner bell summoned her back to reality, and she ran back to the house.

Dinners at the old house were of a formal nature, hearkening back to the days of the professor's youth. Children were not expected to be 'seen and not heard'—not exactly—but the food was rich and the courses were numerous, and the conversation was generally limited to the weather and college affairs. The professor was, this particular evening, discussing his views on the leaking library roof, and aside from Peter's muttered instructions to "blow the whole thing sky-high," it was understood that the children would be all but silent.

Which is why it was so unusual for Julia to break into the conversation. Between the soup and the main course she could no longer contain her curiosity, and asked: "Grandmother, is there any particular reason why the garden outside should glow at night?"

Her grandmother looked at her in astonishment, a fork full of roast beef halfway to her mouth.

"Glow? My dear, your eyes must have been playing tricks on you. Maybe you're feverish! Sometimes people see things when they have a fever." She hurriedly placed a hand on Julia's forehead. "No, no sign of a fever. Dear?" She looked over at her husband. "Is anything wrong with the garden?"

"What's this, my dear?"

The professor was deeply engrossed in his mashed potatoes.

"Julia was wondering why our garden glows at night, dear."

"I have no idea. Does it glow at night? I'd never noticed that. Aha!" He stabbed triumphantly at a pea that had been eluding him.

Julia was not entirely satisfied by her grandfather's reply. "Then could you tell me something about the garden? I mean, how long has it been here?"

"Well, it's all lost in the mists of history, my dear. The garden is one of the oldest parts of Oxford. It was built centuries ago by a—a monk, I believe.

In fact, Julia,"—the professor paused to swallow his peas—"there's an old story about that monk. They say he was murdered in that garden, and he'll never be able to leave it."

Julia's eyes opened very, very wide.

"You mean the garden is haunted?"

Peter guffawed into his water glass. His grandmother intervened quickly.

"Now, dear, we don't want the children getting too excited! I don't want them lying awake at night looking for some ghostly figure in the garden, or worrying that something will creep in through the bedroom window!"

"Of course, of course. You are quite right. Julia, it's just a story. No need to worry! I've never seen any such monk! And—ahem!—neither has anyone else."

And with another *ahem!*, the professor returned to his potatoes.

Julia was sent off to bed early that night. Her grandmother, still not convinced that she wasn't feverish, tucked her in as if she were still a little girl, fluffing her pillows and listening to her prayers. She kissed her forehead and turned out the light, leaving Julia alone with her thoughts. These thoughts primarily concerned

Peter, who was still awake playing with his chemistry set. He was experimenting with gunpowder as usual—the boy was positively obsessed with blowing things up. But Peter was forgotten as her mind once again turned to the garden.

Even from this distance she could almost sense the silver glow. She lay awake, wondering, until the house was dark and silent but for the customary creaks of age. And then she went once more down the stairs and through the creaking door to her garden.

Again she found herself drawn to the pool, guided by the same mysterious force she had felt earlier that evening. She knelt on the grass beside the water, bathed in a ghostly glow, not noticing how the mist from the fountain left a silver stain on her arm. She peered down into it, watching her own reflection. It felt like a gateway. It felt like a beginning.

From deep within the shadows of the trees, a hooded figure watched her. Two children were needed to fulfill the prophecy—when would the other appear?

Peter, reading in bed as usual, heard the hinges wheezing downstairs—Julia had returned from her midnight prowl, he supposed. He closed his Sherlock Holmes novel and laid it on the nightstand. The master detective was once again on the brink of triumph, but triumph would have to wait until tomorrow. Yawning, he got out of bed to close the window. He looked down at the garden below, feeling a bit entranced in a way that was not remotely scientific. So entranced, in fact, that he didn't hear his sister behind him until she spoke.

"Pretty, isn't it?"

He turned and looked at her without recognition until she smiled. He grinned too—the first Julia had seen him really smile in some time. "You've got silver stuff all over you," he pointed out.

"From the fountain," Julia said. She moved over to the window. "You might almost imagine fairies living down there. It feels enchanted, doesn't it?"

"A bit," he agreed, and then caught himself. Enchantment was for girls and children. He gave a harsh laugh. "You've been reading too much *Alice in Wonderland*, Julia," he said. "All that nonsense about pretend worlds. A garden is just a garden. Why do you have to read books that imagine some kind of other world? There's more than enough to explore in this one!"

Julia glared at her brother. "But Peter, what if we were meant to dream dreams? Suppose we had been given the power to dream of other worlds so we could see our own world in a different way?"

"Don't be silly, Julia. We can enjoy gardens without having to believe that fairies live under the trees. Trees are trees, and stars are stars. They're all made up of atoms. So are we, in fact. We're nothing but lots and lots of atoms, and that's all there is to it. There's no enchantment."

Julia flopped on the bed, already frustrated with the familiar conversation. Peter the realist, Peter the scientist, had absolutely *no* imagination. "Surely there's more to it than that, Peter? What if this world is only one of many? You know, like rooms in a building. We're so used to living in only one of them that we don't realize there are others. Better ones, maybe."

Peter yawned, slowly and deliberately. "All right, Julia. Don't work yourself into a fit. I'm sure you'll understand better when you're older, and you won't see fairies or elves or gardens that glow at night."

"You don't see the glow?" Julia asked. "All that silver light—you don't see it?"

"It's the moon, Julia," said Peter, in the patronizing manner of an adult to a young child. Julia was annoyed.

"There's no moon tonight," she announced. "Well, a bit, but just a sliver. Not enough to give that kind of light. Look—" She hopped up and pointed out the window at the dark sky.

And there was nothing for Peter to say.

"Do you see?" Julia asked. "Do you see that it's enchanted?"

"It … it must be …" Peter trailed off, confused. Julia giggled and grabbed his hand.

"Come on, dimwit."

Together they went to the garden — taking care on the creaking stairs not to wake their grandparents — and Julia led him to the pond.

"It's strongest here," she said. "I feel as if it's pulling me."

"It's pulling *us*," said Peter. He shivered — and it was then that he heard his name. It was low, soft — so soft that it might have just been in his mind. But there was an otherworldliness about it that he couldn't quite explain.

He grabbed Julia sharply by the hand and started for the door.

"Julia, we need to get back inside the house. Immediately!" he hissed. "I don't think we're safe here."

But Julia was not listening to Peter. She was staring at the water, and at her reflection within it. The image seemed deeper — stronger somehow. More real than her own face.

"*Julia …*"

That voice again, calling her name. Calling her name, lovingly and gently.

Peter gripped her hand harder, yanking her back towards the doorway. "Come on, Julia. There's something strange going on. We shouldn't be here." There was a note of panic in his voice.

But Julia pulled her hand free. "It's the door, Peter. It's the rabbit hole down to Wonderland, don't you see?"

"*Peter ...*"

"There isn't a Wonderland, there's no enchantment! Come back inside!"

"It's the door, and I have to see what's on the far side. You go back inside if you want to. Don't worry about me." Peter had never heard her sound like this—so adult and serene. Something was changing her ... and changing him too. He seized hold of her hand again but made no attempt to drag her back towards the house and its safety. She lifted her head and smiled at him, and together they stepped into the dark waters.

CHAPTER

3

The warm turquoise sea lapped gently against the deserted white beach, framed by trees swaying slowly and gracefully in the balmy wind. The only sounds to be heard were the quiet swishing and hissing of the water across the sand, and the soft rustling of the trees in the breeze. The sand led right up to a group of grassy dunes, soaking up the warmth of the late afternoon sun.

"Isn't it beautiful?" Julia said dreamily to nobody in particular.

She sat up with a start and rubbed her eyes. She had been asleep and dreaming: it was time to wake up. Yet even as she lowered her hands from her face, she knew that all was not as she expected. The paradise was still there. The blue of the sea and sky were far clearer and brighter than any colors she had ever seen in nature. The only sound she could hear was that of gentle waves swishing over the sand. She was feverish, just as Grandmother had thought.

Julia stood up, alarmed, and then felt the warm breeze tousle her hair. She took a few tentative steps towards the sea, feeling the heat of the sand beneath her feet. There was a curious, dreamlike quality to everything, as if voices had called to her from the world's end over shoreless seas. She must be imagining things, she told herself. Yet it all seemed so real.

She looked down at the sand beneath her toes and, all of a sudden, realized she was barefoot. She hurriedly checked to make sure she was decent. Her mother had always emphasized that proper young ladies should dress modestly. She was relieved to find that she was indeed dressed, but not in her familiar nightgown. She was now wrapped in a white cloth which draped smoothly about her.

Everything seemed wrong. Maybe she had gone mad! Would she be sent to a mental hospital? Wasn't that what had happened to one of her school friend's uncles? He thought (her friend had told her, in the strictest confidence) that he had turned into a seagull, and had tried to fly out the window of his mansion in Kensington. He was now locked up in a special hospital which knew how to deal with people like that. *Oh dear,*

Julia thought to herself. *I may end up meeting him very soon. And I don't think I'd like that very much.*

She took one last look at the bay. She couldn't stay here all day. Somehow she would have to work out where she was and how she could get back home. Shading her eyes, she surveyed the sea stretching into the distance. There was no sign of any ship that might rescue her. She turned to the shore. Each end of the bay was enclosed by rocky promontories, stretching their fingers out into the sea. As she surveyed the scene, Julia noticed a path leading through the woods to her left. A moment later she was walking along it. It led over a small hill to another bay just like the one she had left.

Julia hesitated, then began to walk towards the sand at the end of the path. She might as well have a look at this beach as well. And then she froze in astonishment, mingled with a little fear, because there were footsteps on this beach.

All at once it came to her. The garden, the silver light, the pond ... the pond. The waters had opened up before them and they had found themselves standing on the brink of a chasm, illuminated by a single point of light far, far beneath them. And then they had fallen ...

So where was Peter?

The footsteps seemed to follow a path which wound along the promontory between the bays. She followed the path along the rocky outcrop, woods to her right and sea to her left. Suddenly the trees came to an end and she found herself in a clearing. She could see, hear, and smell the sea through the line of gnarled old trees that encircled the open space. And at the opposite end she saw a familiar figure, his back to her as he looked out over this unfamiliar world. She caught her breath and broke into a run.

Hearing the approaching footsteps, Peter turned. He looked at his sister as she came running towards him and almost didn't recognize her. Her eyes were bright, her face flushed with relief and delight, and he hugged her, something he would never have dreamed of doing back home. But the rules seemed different here.

"Peter, it's come true! We've gotten to Wonderland after all!"

Peter pulled away with a grimace. "I don't think we're in Wonderland, Julia."

"Well then, let's go exploring and find out what this place is." She looked over Peter's shoulder, past the edge of the clearing. "What were you looking at earlier? Did you see anything?"

"I saw a silver patch just over there—no, there," he said, pointing. "It looks just like the light from the garden back at home. I was about to go explore when you appeared."

"It seems as good a place to begin as any," she agreed. "Shall we follow that trail, and see where it takes us?" She indicated a worn path down through the trees.

It might not have been a path at all, as Peter was only too eager to point out. It was nothing more than a deer trail, really—a few patches of trampled grass that wove between the trees. But no other option presenting itself, the two started forward.

And they walked into the woods, the sea receding behind them. The soft whishing of the waves on the shoreline quickly gave way to the rustling of the leafy canopy in the warm breeze. The salty tang of the beach was displaced by the fragrance of blossoms and pine resin. Peter and Julia looked around in wonder at plants which seemed to have come straight out of travelers' tales. Green dappled light flickered on the path ahead of them, while creepers with blue, white, and orange flowers descended on all sides.

"It's magic!" thought Julia to herself.

After ten minutes, the path—if indeed it could be called a path—came to a fork. Peter, in the lead, paused and turned to Julia.

"Which way, do you think?" he asked, scuffing a toe in the ground. He didn't look at his sister, loathe to admit he didn't know the way. Julia, grateful that they had stopped, began ceremoniously tearing wide strips of cloth from the edges of her garment.

"Absolutely no idea," she muttered, teeth clenched as she tore the white cloth. "Wait one minute while I make some shoes. My feet are killing me." She tore off two lengths of fabric and wrapped them carefully around her feet, tucking the ends in under the folds. Peter, seeing the wisdom in this, did likewise.

"Now then," said Julia, grinning at the sight of her brother's freshly swaddled feet, "which path to take?

Where's that silver glow?"

"The trees are blocking it," said Peter. "We've gone downhill from the clearing, I'm afraid." And so they had. There was nothing but forest in every direction, and the two lightly trampled paths leading away from each other.

"Left," said Julia promptly.

"I think right," said Peter.

"Why?"

Peter tried very, very hard to think of a reason, wishing he'd paid a great deal more attention during his Orienteering training as a Boy Scout. He could remember something about the North Star, but it was full daylight, and anyway who was to say that the North Star existed here, wherever they were?

"Because I said so," he concluded. Julia gave a sound somewhere between a snort and a scoff and headed to the left, and what choice had Peter but to follow?

It was a half hour later—a very long half hour later—that the trees fell away to reveal another clearing. The ground sloped steeply down, leading to a level area enclosed by trees that might have been birches but for their silver leaves. On three of the clearing's four sides rakes of seats had been cut into the ground. On the fourth there was a single stone throne. And in the center was a garden—a garden that shone in a silver light all its own.

"Told you it was left," said Julia. Peter noted that

she was smirking—most unnecessarily, he thought. But then he forgot to be annoyed, because really it was the most extraordinary place.

In some ways the garden looked just like the one they had left behind in Oxford. Yet this place was ruined and overgrown with weeds. Peter and Julia walked along an uneven stone pathway, overgrown with thorns and creepers, passing by a stone fountain at the center of the garden. It wasn't working. Grass was growing in its basin and the water spouts seemed to be blocked with mud. The pond was full of weeds and debris. All the stonework had long since been overtaken by a mosaic of lichens and moss, and the trees seemed to have become home to a colony of bats. But in spite of all the ruin and neglect it still had that magical touch of silver about it.

The children were silent for a long moment as they surveyed the desolate scene.

"It's been abandoned for ages," Julia said finally. Peter nodded. He was watching the shadows of the trees lengthen. They were going to be like Hansel and Gretel, lost in a dark forest. There was some shelter to be found in the trees, perhaps, but they had no food, no water, no protection against whatever dangers might lurk in the night. His father would never forgive him if something happened to Julia.

"That pond doesn't feel like another portal, does it?" he asked. Julia shook her head. There was no pull here—no magical presence urging them forward as it had in Oxford.

Peter shivered. The sun was setting, and it was getting cold. Maybe he ought to light a fire. Oh, if only he had paid closer attention in Wilderness Survival!

Julia watched the daylight lose its battle with the encroaching night. Above her, tiny pinpricks of light began to appear in the heavens. She wanted the solemn stillness of this moment to linger forever. It seemed so — well, so significant.

Peter's voice broke into her reverie. "We ought to find shelter," he said.

They found it in the trees. The silver branches of the birches were sturdy and yet pliable, and Peter constructed a sort of canopy under which they could sleep. They would look for water at first light, he decided. Water, and then a way home.

Even without the comfort of a fire he was asleep before Julia. She lay back with her hands behind her head, watching through the branches as the stars winked into the sky. She smiled to herself as she watched them, and the smile stayed on her face as she fell asleep under the silent skies.

CHAPTER

4

Peter woke from a dreamless sleep, his stomach gnawing with hunger. He sat up, rubbed his eyes, and groaned. He had been expecting to wake up in the spare bedroom at his grandparents' home in Oxford. Apparently it hadn't been a dream.

He pushed back the branches and stood, stretching his long limbs. The sun was still low in the sky, but already it had burnt away the chill of the night. It promised to be a hot day. There was one thought in Peter's mind: water.

He bent back under the branches and shook his sister's shoulder. She squirmed under his touch and rolled over with a protesting sigh.

"Julia, we need to find a stream, or some fruit trees or something," he announced. She murmured her agreement and was silent. Peter groaned and shook her again, more forcefully this time. "Julia!"

"Go on; let me sleep," she mumbled. Peter stood and ran a hand through his already tousled hair. He supposed she would be fine there—she was hidden among the tangle of branches, and anyway he could move faster without her. He glanced once more at the sun; they really couldn't wait much longer to find water. He bent down again.

"I'll be back soon, Julia. Don't leave the garden, all right? You promise you'll stay here?"

She nodded through a sleepy haze. Satisfied, Peter headed out of the garden and back to the path, certain that it would lead to a stream.

It was really only a few minutes later—though it felt like much longer—that Julia finally woke to find her brother gone. She extracted herself from the canopy of branches and paced over to the stagnant pond, wondering what Peter had done with himself. She vaguely remembered something about a stream and supposed he had gone off to find water. She debated trying to follow him and concluded that she would do just as well to remain in the garden. There were no predators here—none that she could see, at least.

It was at that moment that she realized she was being watched.

It was some instinct she hadn't known she possessed that warned her of the danger. She stayed very, very still for a long moment, afraid to do so much as breathe. Perhaps if she didn't move, whatever it was would move on. Her eyes darted from side to side, searching for an escape route—or, failing that, some sort of weapon. There were a few mossy stones that had been pushed out of the wall by the sprawling roots of the trees, but they lay too far away to reach. Perhaps if she ran ...

There was really only one thing to do. She turned, slowly and deliberately, and looked the enemy straight in the eye.

It was a man. He stood beside the stone chair, his hands clasped in front of him. He wore a long, hooded robe, and his face was hidden in shadow. And yet Julia could feel his eyes on her. She stood poised and ready to flee, every muscle tensed.

But then he held out a hand to her, and a low, solemn voice said, "Welcome, Julia. We have been waiting a long time for you."

There was a long, wary pause as Julia sized up the stranger.

"Who are you?" she asked cautiously. "What is it that you want of me?"

The man pulled down his hood, and for the first time Julia could see his face. He was old—far older than her grandfather, Julia thought. His face was etched with deep lines—one of them a pink scar running the length of his cheek—and his white hair only thinly covered his scalp. But his eyes were bright, and he was smiling.

"My name is Gaius," he said. "And I want you to fulfill a prophecy."

There was another long moment in which Julia simply stared at the man. He was mad, she thought— mad, and possibly dangerous. She thought again of the stones that lay near the wall and wondered if Peter was nearby. Maybe he would come if she screamed …

"You need not worry," said Gaius. "I have no intention of hurting you. I would like, if you will permit me, to tell you a story."

She nodded, never taking her eyes off his.

"Good," he said. "Now, perhaps I can make you more comfortable?" He gestured to a blanket and cushions spread out on the ground. Julia stared—none of it had been there a moment before. Gaius smiled. "I have a little magic," he said simply.

"Yes … of course," said Julia dumbly. She moved to the blanket and sat down against a cushion, wondering if this was how Alice had felt when she got to Wonderland.

"This is an old story," began Gaius, "and I am the only man yet living who can tell it true. It is the story of a good land and a good people, and how they were brought to ruin."

There was once a country, said Gaius, that lay far beyond the seas. This was a beautiful land, with lush meadows, fragrant woods, and crystal clear rivers dashing down the hills onto the great fertile plains of the south. This land was Khemia, ruled over by Marcus, the crown prince of the Dynasty of Ilium. It was a place of peace, and all its peoples lived in harmony.

It was in the sixth year of Marcus's reign that disaster struck. A dormant volcano erupted, enveloping the land in a blanket of deadly gas released from deep within the earth. Marcus had heard the old stories—stories already ancient in his time—of an island beyond the sea, and organized the evacuation of Khemia. And after six long weeks at sea, weeks without good food or water or space to move, Marcus saw mountains in the distance.

They found themselves in a wild new country—a land of forests and beaches, a land of bright light and mysterious shadows—and set about making a home there. The first crude shelters they built gave way to houses, and the houses to towns, and finally a great castle crowned over the island. It was from this castle that Marcus ruled, and the land grew fertile with justice and peace, just as Khemia had before it.

But there was unrest among the lords. There were whispers in dark rooms and murmurs of treason, which Marcus ignored at his peril. He was an old man by this time, his judgment clouded by the desire for ease and a belief in the loyalty of his people.

His death, some said, was hastened by the hand of one of the lords, but Marcus's health had already been failing and nothing could be proved. The lords took power, three of them crowning themselves regents, and the days of peace were ended. They called themselves the Jackal, the Leopard, and the Wolf, and they enforced their power ruthlessly, enslaving any who refused total obedience to their own selfish ideas and demands. They had been granted unnatural long life by virtue of three ebony amulets which they wore about their necks—and as time went on, they became only more cruel. Marcus's paradise, said Gaius, became a prison.

Julia was quiet throughout the story. She sat with her chin resting on her knees, staring wide-eyed at the man before her. As he fell silent she asked again, in a hushed voice, "Who are you?"

He smiled at her question. "I was with Marcus on Khemia, and I was loyal to him throughout his reign. When the Lords of Aedyn revolted I escaped to these woods. They sent out search parties to try and find me, but they never succeeded. The woods are dark and deep, and are a safe refuge for a fugitive like me."

"And what are we—Peter and I—what are we doing here?"

"I called you," Gaius said simply. "I went to your world and made a way for you to come here."

"The garden," said Julia. "You're the monk—the monk who was ..."

"Murdered," he said grimly. "Yes, I'm the monk. I built the garden as a gateway for the Chosen Ones when the time was right. I was told to call until they heard and answered. And you came."

"Told? Who told you?"

"One even greater than Marcus, child. For there is a greater story—a deeper story. A story which rules all stories. And a story of which you are part."

Julia began to think that someone had made a very big mistake.

"I'm not ... Gaius, I'm not the chosen one. Peter and I ..."

"Who are you to say, my dear, whether or not you are meant for great things?"

Julia shivered.

"Tell me—tell me about this place. Tell me how you can be here if you were—" she swallowed. "If you were murdered back in Oxford."

"I told you before that I have a little magic," said the monk. "Because I died in another world my spirit can remain. And I am needed here to tell the story. The people must not forget. This is where we come to remember." He lifted his head and looked around. "This is the garden of the Great King. It is the place where the faithful have gathered every year for the past five centuries to tell the

story of the exodus from Khemia. And now we also tell
the story of our enslavement in Aedyn."

"Aedyn?"

"This island, fair one. This is Aedyn." Julia nodded as the monk continued. "This garden is where the
faithful gather to remember the past and look forward
to the future. A future ..." He paused. "A future in
which two strangers from another world—the Chosen
Ones—would come to this land and set it free."

"What do you want us to do, Gaius?"

"That is for you to discover. All I can do is tell you
of what has been. I can no longer change things. That is
for you to do. And you will not be alone, fair one. You
will be given a new power to help you fight." He raised
his head, listening. "Your brother comes. I must leave
you." He stood and helped Julia to her feet. "I must warn
you not to speak of this to anyone—not even to your
brother." Julia opened her mouth to protest, and Gaius
put a finger against her lips. "No one may know what
you have learned. Do you understand? You alone know
these truths, and they are dangerous truths indeed. Not
everyone you meet can be trusted."

"But Peter ..."

"You can keep Peter safest by your silence," Gaius
said. "He comes!"

Julia looked around, and then realized that Gaius
was gone. He seemed to have melted into the shadows.

But she was alone for only a moment before a wild-eyed figure appeared from between the trees.

"Peter! You found water?"

"A castle! Julia, there's a castle! Come on!"

Chapter

5

"There!"

Peter pointed triumphantly into the distance. "Over there, through that pass in the mountains."

Julia caught up with him on the crest of a hill and stared into the distance. They edged their way forward into full daylight, making their way onto a large rock. It had steps cut into it, leading up to a kind of platform on its peak. Julia ran up, enthralled by what she saw. The ground fell away sharply beneath the rock to reveal a truly resplendent landscape.

Stretched out in front of them, as far as their eyes could see, was a gentle plain, bathed in the late afternoon sunlight, with rich green fields and hedgerows. There were meadows ahead of her reaching to distant hills, studded with flowers that lent a gentle perfume to the light breeze.

Far away, in the center of the enormous plain, was a great park enclosed by huge, strong walls with fortified gates set at intervals. And at the heart of the park was a castle. Its walls, towers and battlements rose from the plain, glowing in the curious slant of morning sunlight.

Peter turned to her, his eyes flashing with excitement. "It will take us ages to get there but we'll make it. And there's bound to be water along the way—and food when we get to the castle!"

Julia nodded absentmindedly. Food and water ... and whatever Gaius intended his "chosen ones" to do, surely it had to begin at the castle.

They came down from the stone platform and wended their way down a steeply sloping hill. They soon found themselves in the midst of dense forest, but by keeping the mountains in sight whenever they came to a clearing they managed to stay on course. It was not, however, the most comfortable walk they had ever taken. If you have ever slept on hard ground with branches and needles poking into your back and no pillow or blanket, and gone long hours without food or water and then been asked to walk all day without proper shoes ... well, then you have some idea of the mood Peter and Julia were in.

Peter took it better than Julia. He was remembering his time scouting in the woods—remembering

how to walk and how to find a path, and how to avoid
all the little pitfalls that would lead to a twisted ankle.
As he reached the crest of a hill—this one steeper than
most—he looked back to see that Julia had fallen behind. She was tired, he could tell. Her face was red from
the exertion and she was breathing hard, and her hands
were muddy from where she'd fallen and caught herself.

He took a low branch from a nearby tree and
snapped it off cleanly at the trunk. By the time Julia had
caught up with him he'd stripped it of all its twigs and
leaves, and he thrust it at her without a word.

"What's this?" she asked, puzzled.

"A walking stick," he said. "It'll help on the hills."
She nodded and grasped it.

"Thank you."

Those were the only words that passed between
them for some time. There wasn't much to say. When
the path was even and Julia didn't need to concentrate
so much on the terrain she wondered about her brother.
There was something odd in his eyes, she thought.
Something new. For lack of a better word she called it
determination, but she thought, when she cast a sideways glance at him, that it was something more than
that. But then the terrain would change again, and she
would need to focus on her steps instead of pondering
the many mysteries of Peter. And so they walked on, the
castle always ahead, going more slowly now that the sun

was high in the sky and beating down on them.

They reached the mountain pass in the early afternoon. The woods ended suddenly, as if someone had drawn a line beyond which trees were not permitted to transgress. Ahead of them were meadows, verdant with all kinds of grains, trees, and flowers. There was no sign of birds or any animals. In England, Peter thought to himself, surely pastures like this would be filled with cows and sheep, grazing contentedly on this rich grass, perhaps peering at them through gates as they passed. Or maybe plough horses would be tossing their heads, ready to begin work in the fields. Yet all that met his eye was a vast expanse of golds and greens, stretching far into the distance.

The plain ahead of them was divided up like a checkerboard into fields, each surrounded by hedges studded with bright flowers. The heads of the golden grain swayed gently in the warm breeze in some of these fields; others were dotted with all kinds of fruit trees, their branches heavy with the rich and ripening fruit. Julia gave a little cry of delight at the sight of them and, casting aside her walking stick, found the energy to run.

In later years Julia would try to describe that fruit and never quite managed it. None of it was like anything she'd ever had in England—the flavors were richer and deeper, the colors bolder, and the juice infinitely more refreshing. They ate until the liquid ran down their faces

and hands and stained their tunics, and then they looked
at each other and laughed.

It was the first that either of them had really
laughed since arriving in Aedyn, and it felt absolutely
magnificent. Nothing was particularly funny, but the relief and pleasure at finding the fruit was simply beyond
compare. They laughed until the tears came, until they
had to hold their stomachs for fear of bursting. And it
was when the laughter had passed and they were lying
on the ground, grinning at each other, that Julia heard
the stream.

She would likely never have heard it had there
been noises from animals, but in the clear air the sound
was unmistakable. She sat up and stared.

"Is that—Peter, is that water?"

"Where?"

She listened very hard.

"Over there." She pointed over her shoulder to
the left. "Beyond that line of trees. I'm ... yes, I'm certain
it's a stream."

Peter was on his feet and bounding towards the
trees in seconds, Julia following close after him. They
didn't need water quite as desperately as they had before they'd found the fruit trees, but they were both still
thirsty and a long walk remained ahead of them.

They fell upon the stream like a lion on its prey.
The water was cold and clear and they drank until they

could drink no more. And then Julia splashed Peter—an accident, she insisted—and Peter splashed back, and soon both of them were drenched through. They lay back on the bank of the stream, letting the hot sun dry them. They spoke of nothing in particular—school, friends, their father—and then they fell silent for a long moment.

"I wonder what we'll find at the castle," Julia said, finally breaking the silence.

"A way home, perhaps?" replied Peter dryly. "I daresay we'll find someone there who can explain all this to us—how we got here and why we're here and how we can get back to Oxford."

"You don't—" Julia paused. "You don't think there might be work for us to do here? Some reason for us to have been called? I mean—maybe it's not time for us to go home yet."

Peter gave her a very hard look. "I suppose we'll find out," he said. "In the meantime, we'd better keep moving."

They made their way back to the field in the mountain pass. Some rough trails led through the waving grasses, all pointing them—or so it seemed to Peter—to the great castle in the distance, raised up from the surrounding land. He chose the trail that seemed most direct and they started forward.

Refreshed from the fruit and water and with the

help of Julia's new walking stick, they were able to move much more quickly than before. It was perhaps twenty minutes before Julia stopped dead in her tracks.

"Oh, honestly," said Peter through his teeth. "We'll never make it if ..." But he never finished his sentence, transfixed by the sight of his sister. Her eyes were wide with something like fear, and one finger pointed off to the east. Peter followed her gaze and saw them.

There were three men on horseback, following what he imagined to be another one of the paths to the castle. They were clad in black and hooded—even from this distance he could tell that their faces were covered. Something in their posture indicated that these were not friends. A chill went through the air, and the sun seemed to shine a little less brightly overhead as Peter finally understood: they were patrolling.

"Get down," Julia breathed. "We need to find cover." They looked around sharply—there were no trees for a mile, and the long grasses had given way to a field of wildflowers barely six inches high. This place would do little to hide them.

"Over there," said Peter slowly, nodding his head back the way they'd come. "Get back into the tall grass, and with any luck ..."

But it was already too late. The horsemen had seen them, and as one they shifted course, heading straight for Peter and Julia.

They tried to run, of course. Every instinct urged them forward, though it was hopeless from the beginning—who could ever outrun those stallions?

They were upon them in moments. Peter, in a last, desperate effort to conceal himself, flung himself into the long grass and tried to crawl away. Julia turned to face the horsemen and screamed with all her might—not out of fear, but rage.

No one was more startled by the result than she.

The scream that came from her lips wasn't the high-pitched shriek of a young girl, but a sound infinitely stronger and deeper. It knocked the horsemen from their stallions and, far away, shook the leaves from the trees. Peter clapped his hands over his ears and moaned, the horses fled with panicked whinnies, and Julia, the cold rage still in her eyes, clenched her fists and screamed harder. She didn't understand it—didn't know where this voice was coming from—but she knew that the sun was shaking in the sky and that the three hooded figures were in pain.

They were writhing, hands hard over their ears, desperate to get away but paralyzed by the screaming. As Julia stopped for breath they moaned and rolled over, and then were still.

She paused, breathing hard, and looked back at her brother. He was staring at her as if she were a stranger —some unearthly apparition. She put out a hand to help him up.

"How … what …"

"I don't know," she said bluntly. "Let's get going before they wake up."

Peter, never one to disagree with a girl whose screams could shake the sun, stood up and followed.

It was a very quiet walk. Julia was lost in her own private contemplation, and Peter was sneaking sideways glances at her. That screaming had not been normal, he thought. Something had happened to her—something horrible, probably. He longed to get to the castle, certain that all the mysteries of this place would be explained as soon as they arrived.

The castle wasn't far away now. It dominated the horizon, raised up from the surrounding meadows as if it had risen from the earth in order to rule everything around it. Maybe they have cannons up on the ramparts, Peter thought to himself. If they had enough gunpowder, they could control the entire plain.

Surrounding the castle itself was a yellow stone wall. They followed it for what seemed like ages until they came to a great wooden gate. Its planks were old, studded with nails and rot, but the gate was sturdy. Peter gave it a few kicks to no avail.

"What happens now?" Julia whispered.

"I've no idea," he muttered. "Why don't you try that screaming? Maybe it'll knock the door in."

This proved unnecessary, however, when the massive gate began to swing open with a solemn, creaking slowness. Peter and Julia looked at each other, shrugged, and entered.

CHAPTER

6

Once inside the wall they were able to see who had opened it: a tall figure swathed in dark robes. They couldn't see the face, and at first they both thought it was another one of the riders who had been on patrol in the mountain pass. But this figure was different—sunken, somehow, and lacking the raw power of the riders. The man—if it was a man—was silent as he pointed up towards the castle.

Peter found himself overwhelmed with the immensity of the building: it was more majestic, more splendid, than any castle he had seen on earth. Even Windsor Castle (which he had once visited on a school trip) seemed to pale into insignificance alongside this great construction.

As they walked along the path changed to cobbled

streets, flanked on either side by a series of low houses. The old stone buildings were covered with climbing plants rising high on each side. Each house had its own brightly colored door, but the paint was fading in places and patches of bare wood showed through where it had splintered off altogether. The doors and shutters were all closed tight, and Julia realized with a shudder that it was as completely silent here in the town as it had been back in the meadow. There were no people out at work—no women hanging laundry, no men whistling as they went about their chores, no children playing in the streets. In a curious impulse Julia reached out and took Peter's hand, holding it tight as they walked.

The cobbled street led slowly uphill, passing through an open gate. They came to a stop in a court-yard—a courtyard as empty as the streets. An immense stone staircase at the opposite end of the square led up to a grand doorway—the entrance to the castle—but both children hesitated.

"It feels a bit haunted," said Julia. Peter nodded and squeezed her hand.

"Everything's felt haunted so far. Come on."

Together they ascended the staircase. When they reached the door, Peter put out his hand and knocked.

For a moment there was complete silence, as if the world was holding its breath. Then they heard a slow creaking and the door swung outwards. With their eyes accustomed to the bright sunlight they could see only darkness indoors, but after a moment they distin-guished two figures.

Someone was coming out.

The two figures descended toward them pur-posefully, swords in their belts. They were dressed in gray robes, their faces hidden by hoods. Julia, who had recently written a well-received school essay on Francis of Assisi, thought they looked like Franciscan monks. (Or were they friars? She was a little vague on that point.) But where were their faces? It was as if the uniform was designed to hide their identities—just like the horsemen back in the meadow and the silent figure at the gate.

Peter was terrified by the sight of the men. If they were men at all. Their robes concealed so much that it was impossible to tell if they were even human. But he watched as the figures bowed, gestured towards them, and stood to the side, allowing them to pass into the castle. Peter glanced at Julia and she at him, and together they passed through the open doorway into a great, vaulted antechamber. It was dimly lit, and they both stumbled on a low stone step as they entered. But as their eyes adjusted they could make out guards and courtiers standing at attention along the columned walls. And at the far end, three thrones were set on a raised platform.

Peter heard a sharp intake of breath beside him, and he nearly stumbled again when he saw what had startled Julia. On the thrones sat three hooded figures, and where their faces ought to have been there were masks, gilded and embellished with mysterious symbols. They were like the animal gods of ancient peoples, he thought. The central figure wore the mask of a wolf, and the other two the masks of a leopard and jackal.

Julia shivered, remembering Gaius's story in the garden. The Jackal, the Leopard, and the Wolf—the three lords who had overthrown Marcus. She stared, transfixed, at the masks' dark, empty slits from behind which she knew eyes were watching her. A shiver shot down her spine, leaving a tingling of anxiety behind.

They regarded each other for a long moment, and then one of the courtiers, swathed in a wine-red robe, marched to the center of the chamber and turned toward Peter and Julia. They were not surprised to find themselves staring at an oval darkness enclosed by a hood. The courtier gave a menacing snarl.

"You stand in the presence of the three Lords of Aedyn. Declare your business. Who are you? Why are you here?"

Peter was tongue-tied. He didn't imagine that it would be at all helpful to splutter "My name is Peter and I want to go home," but what other answer was there? He was searching for a way to explain that didn't make him sound like a fool when Julia finally spoke up.

She too had been frightened, and unable to think of any explanation for their presence in Aedyn beyond "A ghost called us here to overthrow you, sir." She couldn't take her eyes from those hideous masks. But then, all at once, she remembered her father—remembered him pacing back and forth in her mother's parlor and practicing his grand speeches. She moved forward two paces, bowed, and spoke in a deep, confident voice that she did not recognize as her own.

"My lords, I am Julia of Londinium, the emissary of the Emperor of Albion, a great and powerful land beyond the boundless western sea. This is Lord Peter, my trusted counselor and advisor. We bear greetings from our great Emperor, who asks that we might discuss matters of mutual interest and concern."

She bowed, and the lord with the mask of a wolf nodded.

"Albion," he said. "It must be a long distance indeed if your travels have been so ... disagreeable." He motioned pointedly at the torn and dirty rags that compromised Peter and Julia's clothes.

"A shipwreck," Julia said hastily. "I apologize for appearing before you in this manner. We were"—she glanced at her brother—"the only survivors." The lords murmured their understanding.

Peter watched Julia in utter astonishment. Was this really his sister? Where did she learn to speak like that? Couldn't she just have asked them the way to the mystic portal that led back to Oxford? He watched anxiously as the three Lords of Aedyn conferred together. There appeared to be some sort of disagreement taking place, and he was tempted to run for his life. Yet he knew that the doors to the great chamber had been closed after they had entered. They had no option other than to wait.

After a few moments, the lord with the mask of a wolf turned toward them and beckoned to them to approach. Peter, watching Julia out of the corner of his eye, stepped forward alongside her and bowed before the thrones. Then the lord spoke in a low, hissing voice which chilled his blood.

"Lady Julia, you and Lord Peter are most welcome here in Aedyn. I am the Wolf, the great lord of this country, and these—" he gestured grandly to the other lords—"are my colleagues, the Jackal and the Leopard. Together, we rule this island." There was a hint of a pause in which Julia imagined that he might, underneath his mask, be giving a venomous smile. "We have long believed that there was some great land beyond the seas, but we did not know its name, nor its location. We will learn more of your land, and we can discuss how we might be of help to each other in this difficult world. You will join us tomorrow in the Great Hall, when we can speak more fully and frankly. In the meantime," he raised his voice and spread his arms, "you are our guests. All we have will be at your disposal throughout your time in Aedyn." The Wolf looked to the side and nodded almost imperceptibly at someone in the shadows, then returned to his throne. The audience was over.

Julia murmured her thanks and bowed, relieved beyond measure. She and Peter turned and walked away, feeling almost as if they had escaped. When they reached the back of the great hall, another courtier dressed in red robes greeted them and led them out by a side door. His face, they were almost startled to see, was unmasked. He was not an old man but he was no longer young, and his eyes were not kind.

"I am Anaximander," he told them, "the Lord Chamberlain of Aedyn, and I give you greetings. You will be taken to your chambers by two slaves, where you will be provided with food and water for bathing and," he said, looking pointedly at the torn and muddy cloth in which they were dressed, "some decent clothing."

Anaximander gestured toward two faceless figures dressed in black robes and hoods. "If you need anything, ask them, and they will provide it."

"Thank you, Anaximander." Julia smiled and bowed her head politely. "Might I ask the names of these servants?"

"Slaves don't have names," he said dismissively. "Please don't trouble yourselves about such trivial matters. Rest, and enjoy Aedyn's hospitality." Julia saw that he was smiling — a smile she didn't quite trust.

"Thank you, Anaximander. We will look forward to our meeting with the Lords of Aedyn tomorrow."

After a further exchange of bows Julia and Peter were led away by the two slaves, who guided them silently through the corridors of the castle. They ascended a marble staircase and were shown into a set of rooms with a magnificent view of the island's central plain. Food and drink was already laid out for them there, and after the slaves had departed with low bows, they picked at the meal tentatively. Peter was the first to break the silence.

"Julia, what on earth is going on? Why did you

say we were emissaries? Why didn't you ask them about getting home?"

"Because …" Gaius's warning came into her mind. Peter couldn't know everything—not yet. He couldn't know that the lords would most likely have them killed if they didn't make themselves seem important. "Because I think there's work for us to do here, and we won't be able to get home until we've done it."

Peter was more than a little annoyed by this answer, but his frustration was forgotten when the two silent slaves reappeared, each carrying bottles of perfumes and oils. They were ushered into rooms with tubs full of steaming water and invited to soak as long as they desired, and in such a situation perhaps they can both be forgiven for forgetting about their plight and the meeting the next day.

And so Peter and Julia rested in their chambers, unaware that their fate was being decided far below.

The three Lords of Aedyn were, at that very moment, sitting around a table, the remnants of dinner on the plates before them and wine still in their glasses. The Wolf had his glass in his hand, swirling the contents around and around as he considered. The others were silent—their arguments had been made, and it was left to the Wolf to make the final decision. Finally, he spoke, the echoes of his hissing rasp lingering within the room.

"We will meet these fair strangers tomorrow. If we cannot use them, we will destroy them. Let us hope that they sleep well," he said, smiling beneath his mask. "It may be their last night alive."

Chapter

7

Peter woke with the dawn the next morning, opening his eyes to see light streaming through the window. He threw off the bedclothes and stretched, yawning deeply. No matter how menacing the Lords and their castle might be, they certainly knew how to make a guest comfortable. Peter was not one to decry the pleasures of a warm, soft bed, especially after a night spent on the ground and a long walk over rough terrain.

He looked around him and noticed that the ragged, dirty cloth he had arrived in had been replaced by a set of clothing fit for a prince. He fingered the rich material, noting with some surprise that a twist of paper lay atop the breast pocket.

He picked it up and turned it over in his hand, finally realizing that it contained a handful of gunpowder.

He'd forgotten about it until now—two nights ago, back in Oxford, he'd been experimenting with his chemistry set when his grandmother had announced that it was high time he get to bed. He'd scooped up the product of his experiment and twisted it into a bit of paper, then shoved it in his pocket and forgotten about it. Strange—that his original clothing had been replaced by a white robe, but this bit of powder had come along into this world.

He changed quickly, pausing only to admire himself in the mirror, and shoved the gunpowder back into his pocket. One never knew when that sort of thing might be handy. Science—now there was something one could rely on. Nothing chancy or magical about science, was there? And then, deciding that he was going to do some investigation and clue collecting, just like Sherlock Holmes, and figure out all the mysteries of this place, he went to go find Julia.

She was already awake and dressed when he got there—awake and dressed and ready for business. She'd been wondering exactly what was going to happen at this meeting in the Great Hall and how on earth they were going to maintain this ruse about being emissaries from Albion, and, to that end, had already written the beginnings of a list.

"Oh good, you're up," she said tersely. "Sit down and help."

Peter did as indicated.

"Now: our object is to overthrow the lords and free the slaves." She indicated this written at the top of her list. "So ..."

"Pardon me?" said Peter. She looked up.

"What's wrong?"

"That's our object?" he said incredulously. "How do we know that's our object?"

"Because ..." She thought again of the garden, and the monk's warning that Peter could be kept safest through his ignorance. "Because this isn't how it should be. Slaves and tyrannical lords and all that."

"We don't know that they're tyrannical, Julia."

"What do you think they are—benevolent? With those horrible masks? The Jackal and the Leopard the and Wolf?"

"I don't know, and that's just the point." Peter paused for a moment, looking very puffed up and pleased with himself. "We have to use reason here. Observation. Look for facts, and use them to draw our conclusions."

"Oh, honestly." Julia slammed her list down on the table in a huff. "Truth isn't always logical, you know."

"Of course it is," Peter said smugly. "I thought I'd start in the library—you know, do some reading on this place's history."

Julia was about to say something snide and possibly regrettable about her brother's capacity for reason

when they were both startled by a knock on the door.
Before either of them could answer the door swung open
to reveal a red-robed, bejeweled figure: Anaximander.

"Our Lords of Aedyn request your presence," he
said grandly, and with a sweeping gesture stepped aside
and indicated the door. Peter and Julia rose and followed
him, glaring at each other just for good measure.

The Great Hall was empty but for the lords, whose
masks were no less imposing than they had been the
previous day. Peter and Julia went forward and bent
down in a low bow, Julia quietly gritting her teeth.

"Welcome, my lord and lady," said the Wolf.
"Come, tell us something of your land. Tell us of Albion."

Peter looked at Julia. Julia looked at Peter. He
shrugged almost imperceptibly, and so she began.

"My lords, the great nation of Albion lies far over
the western seas. Our great Emperor wishes to establish
peace and mutual prosperity throughout this region. We
offer assurances of security. In return, we ask for your
guarantee of neutrality and non—" What was her father's word? "Non-aggression."

The Wolf listened patiently as Julia outlined her

proposal, his long, pale fingers pressed together at their tips. He nodded as she finished, and touched his fingers to a dark amulet that lay against his robes.

"My Lady Julia, we are indeed honored that the Emperor of Albion should take notice of such a small nation as Aedyn. Might I ask what led you to single us out for the special favor of your visit? It seems vastly in excess of our size and importance, if I may be forgiven for saying so."

"We did not wish to omit you when we consulted with our neighbors, my lord. It is our hope to build friendship with all nations, great and small, and to … to share our knowledge with each other." Julia smiled, trying to think fast. By now she had exhausted every item on the list she'd made earlier that morning and had absolutely no idea what to say next.

"Share knowledge?" The Wolf leaned forward.

"Yes," said Julia with a noncommittal smile. She was trying desperately to sound like an emissary—trying to sound like someone who was too important to execute—but she was out of ideas. She glanced at Peter, trying to privately indicate desperation.

"Like this, my lord," said Peter, reaching into his breast pocket. "See here a small example of our skills!"

Julia couldn't quite make out what it was that Peter had in his hand. He crossed the hall to an enormous candelabra and held whatever it was to the flame, then threw it down in the lords' direction.

The room exploded, the detonation reverberating throughout the enclosed space. Acrid smoke filled the room, and as it cleared Julia could see the three lords cowering before their thrones in positions of abject terror. The Leopard was coughing violently, trying to waft away the choking fumes, and the Jackal had his hands clasped firmly on his ears. The Wolf rose first, and pointed a shaking finger at Peter.

"What was that devil in your hand?" he hissed.

Guards were now pouring into the hall, swords drawn against the unknown enemy. The Wolf waved them away with a few quick words, never taking his eyes from Peter. There was a long silence.

"What have you to say for yourself, boy?" he spluttered. "What black magic is that in your fingertips?"

Julia noted at this point that Peter was looking rather smug. She disliked this intensely, and wished she could have a moment to consult with Peter before he said something really stupid. But Peter was looking directly at the hideous mask which hid the face of the Wolf, and spoke slowly and with authority.

"My lord, that is a very small example of our power. This room and this castle would be destroyed, along with everyone inside them, were I to demonstrate the true power that Albion commands. It is called gunpowder."

There was not a great deal to say after that. The emissaries had shown their superior hand, the lords were quaking in their boots, and Julia was feeling more than a little apprehensive. She made a great show of bows and smiles and good wishes and fairly dragged Peter out of the hall.

"That went well, I thought!" he said when they'd returned to their chambers.

"Well! Gunpowder! Weapons beyond their comprehension! Oh, marvelous, marvelous indeed!" Julia paced the room.

"You said the object was to overthrow them."

"I don't know what we're supposed to do, but it certainly didn't involve an explosion in the Great Hall!"

Julia was very close to tears, and it may have turned into a nasty fight indeed had Julia not at that moment realized that she'd left her cloak in the Great Hall. It had lain loosely about her shoulders and, when she had flung herself to the side during the explosion, it had fallen off. She hated to leave it down there where it might be trampled on and she wanted an excuse to get Peter out of her sight, so she announced shortly that she would return soon and fled the chamber.

She stalked moodily down the corridors and down the massive flights of stairs, wishing a little desperately that she had never seen a silver glow in the garden. She didn't know what to do or how to rescue any slaves—and, at the moment, didn't see any reason why she ought to bother. And Peter, throwing around tough words and explosions when he didn't understand what was going on … Peter was just impossible.

It was in such a mood that she once again reached the Great Hall.

Something stopped her from entering—even from knocking. There were voices within. She pressed her ear to the door and listened intently, struggling to hear what they were saying. One voice was dominant—a menacing hiss that she immediately recognized as the Wolf.

"But there is still the risk of revolt from the slaves to deal with," he was saying. "The scouts are still hearing rumors of runaway slaves in the great forest of the west. You will recall that the detachment of guards we sent to find them two months ago never came back, and I fear …" There was a long pause. "I fear those slaves in the forest could be the nucleus of a revolt."

Another, more rasping, voice took over the conversation. The Jackal.

"But with this new weapon we can destroy those slaves in the forest. It will be the end of any revolt!"

"The slaves are not stupid," agreed a third voice.

"They'll fall into line as soon as we show our strength. We're safe."

Julia could hear the unmistakable sound of wine being poured from a bottle into glasses, followed by sounds of clinking and coarse laughter. She had heard enough. She melted back into the shadows and retraced her steps to the bedchamber.

CHAPTER

8

Peter watched Julia go with a sense of relief. There had been nothing at all wrong with showing off the gunpowder—nothing wrong with demonstrating that he was a force to be reckoned with.

He stalked brusquely out of the room and stomped down the corridors. Girls! What use were they—so emotional, so unscientific! He would show her! He would figure out the riddle of this place!

He stopped a robed figure in the halls and asked the way to the library. He was pointed silently towards the north tower of the castle, and, after a few minutes of searching through dark and dusty corridors, he happened upon it.

The library he found could have graced an English country house, but it was far grander and more

magnificent. Books were stacked as far up as the eye
could see, shelves upon shelves of them—books on every topic imaginable. Peter looked up and up and up,
breathing in the leather-bound scent of it all.

There was a short "ahem!" and a clearing of the
throat somewhere to his right, and Peter glanced around.
Seated at an enormous oak desk was a thin, bespectacled
man who could only be the librarian.

Peter approached him slowly, trying to size him
up. He noted his ink-stained fingers, the pencil behind
his right ear, and a large leather book full of annotations
on his desk. The man looked irritated at the intrusion.
It seemed, Peter thought to himself, that the library did
not have a great many users.

"Well? What do you want? I'm very busy at the
moment, so make it quick."

"I'm Peter," he said simply. "From … from
Albion." He caught himself stumbling and tried to sound
a great deal grander. "I was wondering if I might look
around for just a bit."

The librarian peered over his spectacles at him,
his alert eyes evaluating him. "You are most welcome,"
he said carefully. "Can I—ahem! Can I be of help to you
in any way?"

"Well, I had hoped to learn something of the history of this island. It might help me understand it better." Peter squared his shoulders and tried to look taller.

"For diplomatic purposes, of course."

"Of course." The librarian stood—he really wasn't much taller standing than sitting—and moved out from behind the desk. "There is a reading desk over here with a wonderful view over the island. Nobody will bother you there. Would you like me to bring you any books? Or would you prefer to look for some yourself?"

"Oh, I'd be delighted if you brought me anything that might be helpful." Peter folded his hands behind his back and tried to look important as he waited. After a moment the librarian reappeared, a worn leather tome in his hand. He handed it to Peter with a smile that he couldn't quite interpret and returned to his annotating.

Peter went to a desk and settled in to read.

The book told a simple story. Aedyn had originally been a wild, untamed island, ruled by a backward and oppressive king. And then came the revolution.

It was called the Illumination. The island had been taken over by a small but determined group of people—determined and highly intelligent. Their rebellion against the feudalism and backward ways of previous generations was led by three lords—the Jackal, the Leopard, and the Wolf—who had established themselves as the enlightened rulers of the island. The old king had been deposed, and later died in exile. Some of the population remained loyal to the old ways and were allowed to remain on the island only on condition of serving the new rulers. But the island, ruled by the same great lords for five hundred years — five hundred years! Was that possible? — had overcome its barbaric beginnings and was now prosperous and forward-looking.

Peter smiled to himself as he read, not hearing the footsteps as they approached — not sensing anyone beside him until a cold hand came down and gripped his shoulder.

"Some light reading, I see!" said a voice. Peter whipped around to see Anaximader right standing behind him.

"Oh — yes," said Peter. "Just some — yes, I was wondering about Aedyn, and ..." he suddenly remembered that he was supposed to sound important. "And its history, culture, chief exports and trade — you know the sort of thing."

"A good choice," replied Anaximander, taking the book from Peter and turning it over in his hands. He flipped through a few of the yellowed pages, looking contemplative. "An important book — an important history for the citizens of Aedyn to keep always in their minds." He trailed off, then looked back up at Peter. "That's what education is about, after all! Protecting ourselves from delusions, preventing innocent minds from becoming corrupted."

"I was reading about the Illumination," said Peter. "Don't — I mean, do the people still have these delusions in Aedyn?"

"I regret that they do," said Anaximander slowly. "The slaves—you've seen them—are very backward. They believe in all sorts of superstitious nonsense."

"Such as?"

"Magic," Anaximander said. "Divine magic. And old, old stories—just fairy tales, really. Stories to explain things they couldn't understand."

This all made a great deal of sense to Peter. It was like Julia, telling herself stories and turning to her books whenever she was confused or upset. He nodded. "You're a people of science," he said. Anaximander granted him a smile.

"We are. And it is for that reason that I come to you." Anaximander pulled over a chair and sat to face Peter. "The lords were most impressed by the invention that you showed them yesterday. The lords said you had a devil in your hand—something you called gunpowder. Did you make it yourself?" His eyes were inquisitive.

"I did." Peter got a look on his face that he intended to be appropriately humble, but which Julia would have recognized as smug. "Of course, the precise formula is a secret known only to me—and the other great minds of Albion, of course."

Anaximander smiled. "Of course, Lord Peter. The Jackal, the Leopard, and the Wolf are most favorably impressed by your abilities. Not only are you a man of great intelligence, but you have shown great wisdom and distinction." He dipped his head in a brief bow.

"You flatter me, sir," said Peter, who really was quite flattered. Anaximander smiled again.

"I do not seek to flatter you, Lord Peter. I only tell you what I observe and what I myself have been told. The Lady Julia spoke of sharing knowledge, and I confess that our great lords are most eager to learn more of your secrets."

"The secrets are not mine to give," started Peter, but Anaximander leaned in closer and breathed softly in his ear.

"The lords would make you a prince of this land." He drew out the word "prince," letting it roll, sparkling, over his tongue. The sound of it filled Peter with glittering images—images foreign to the lonely life of a schoolboy he'd left behind in England. Images of glory, of riches, of dominion over everyone who had teased and brutalized him at school. His eyes were wide and his gaze was far away. Anaximander brought him back to the moment by repeating the word.

"A prince, Peter."

Peter's eyes snapped back to the red-robed figure before him. "Gunpowder is simple, really," he said, and, grasping a quill laid out on the table, sketched a brief formula on a sheet of paper. He passed it to Anaximander, who smiled as he took it in his hand.

"Aedyn is fortunate indeed to have such a wise leader to guide it into the future!" He rose and bowed low, then turned on his heel and left the library.

Peter returned to his own apartment in high spirits. He was walking on air, delighted at being part of such a wise and advanced civilization. A prince of this civilization!

Julia was still shaking as she returned to the bedchamber. As she walked she mulled over the conversation she had just overheard—a rebellious band of slaves, a new weapon to defeat them … and then there were the two Chosen Ones, called from another world. This was all becoming exceptionally difficult.

She flopped onto the bed, wondering if a good cry might help and determining that tears were probably beneath an emissary of Albion. Oh, it was all wrong, she'd messed it all up! She never should have pretended, never should have come here in the first place, never should have paid attention to that wretched monk in the garden!

And then, in spite of all her determination, the tears came after all. She heaved great, noisy sobs into the pillows, gasping as hot tears poured out of her eyes.

And it was at this moment that the slaves came in to lay out the afternoon meal.

Some people have been given the great gift of looking pretty when they cry. They become all the more lovely as delicate tears stream gently down their cheeks. Julia was not one of these fortunate few. Her blonde hair was plastered messily to one side of her face and the other lined with the folds of the blankets. Her cheeks were a bright, splotchy pink and her eyes a deeply unfortunate red.

The slaves of the castle had been absolutely forbidden, on pain of death, to speak with the fair strangers. But when confronted with such an unfortunate sight—with a young woman who has suddenly been transformed into a very young, very unhappy girl, their orders ceased to mean a thing. They both started forward, the taller of the two grasping Julia into a hard embrace.

The slave, a woman, smelled of the same fruit Julia had encountered in the meadow beyond the mountain pass, and she was unaccountably reminded of her mother. She buried her face into the slave's shoulder and gave a few shuddery breaths as she tried to stop crying and look presentable.

"I'm … I'm so sorry," she started, and then she looked up. The slave who was holding her had let her hood fall back, and her face could be plainly seen. It was deeply lined and her dark hair was streaked with gray, but she was not, Julia thought, an old woman. Her eyes were deep-set but clear, and there was a hint of youth left in them.

The woman smiled, and Julia noted that at least a few of the lines in her face came not from the rigors of hard work but from laughter. "I'm Helen," she said simply. "Now, why don't you tell us what's troubling you?"

There was a sharp intake of breath from the other slave, and a look between the two of them that Julia barely registered. The second slave let her breath out in a hiss and nodded almost imperceptibly. "I don't know what to do," Julia said, wiping her face and nose on her sleeve. "The monk said there was a prophecy—said I—we—were the Chosen Ones and I ought to free you, but I don't even know where to begin!"

Another look between the slaves—this one longer and more pronounced. Helen finally broke the silence.

"A monk told you about a prophecy?" she asked slowly. Julia nodded.

"And I'm not to tell Peter, but I think he's already ruined everything with his silly gunpowder and I don't know how to overthrow the lords and I'm out of ideas!"

The second slave removed her hood and stepped forward. She was quite a young woman—not much older than Julia herself, though with a hard look in her eye that could only have come from years of hard work and pain. "If you are the one who was promised us," she said, "you will not have to overthrow them alone." She paused, and then broke into a smile. "I'm Alyce," she said. "Our people have been waiting for you a long, long time, my lady."

It was her smile that finally brought Julia out of her tears and into the moment. Whether or not she was really the Chosen One, she was the only one here. And she had to do something.

"Would you ..." she paused, uncertain exactly how to phrase her question. "Would you tell me your stories? Tell me your history. Tell me of Marcus and all the others."

Helen nodded. "Of course, my lady, but now is not the time. I will arrange for you to meet with my brother, and he will tell the tale true. But first, I feel you must know what you risk." She stopped and glanced at Alyce, who nodded, urging her to continue. "You must understand that by siding with us your life is forfeit. The lords ..." Again she hesitated. "The Wolf is not known for his mercy."

Julia nodded, not precisely sure how to respond. And then Alyce smiled again. She came to Julia's side and held her face, still red and wet from the tears, between her hands. "Welcome, Julia," she said softly. "Welcome to Aedyn."

CHAPTER

9

That afternoon, Julia slipped out of her chambers and made her way down the stairs and through the dark corridors to the slaves' meeting place, following Helen's directions. The tapestries hanging on the walls became more and more dusty and threadbare as she went, and there was a dank, musty smell in the air as she descended into the bowels of the castle. But she held her head high, stepping briskly and with confidence, trying to look as if she had every right in the world to be there.

She need not have worried. Nobody noticed or challenged her. Julia found the door that Alyce had described and opened it, trying not to let it creak. She shivered—the air had a wet chill here, and there was a steady drip from somewhere to the left. She minced her

way down a spiral stone staircase into what was clearly the basement of the castle. The fragrance of a cooking stew wafted through the dark stone cellars, mingling with the less pleasant smells of stagnant water and rotting food. She could see only by the flickering light of the torches burning at intervals, and she guided herself by running her fingers along the wall, shuddering as she felt the muck and slime beneath them.At last she found herself in what looked like an old wine cellar, with wooden benches arranged against its walls. And on the benches sat a small group of hooded figures, huddling together for warmth in the cold, dank air. They stood as she entered the room.

One stepped forward. He was of a muscular build, and might have been a soldier or warrior had he not been born into slavery. His eyes were dark and hard and, like Helen's, set deeply into his face.

"Greetings, Lady Julia. I am Simeon. You have already met Helen and Alyce, and these are a few of the others—more of those who have been enslaved by the Wolf and his men." Julia nodded her head in a brief gesture of greeting, then sat down on the cold bench where Simeon indicated.

"I am very grateful to you—to all of you," she said carefully. "Please tell me about yourselves. Gaius told me so little in the garden, and I … I want so much to understand."

Simeon smiled. "Of course, lady Julia. Let me

begin by telling you how we came to be slaves."

Julia had already heard something of the story he told, but he explained everything more fully than Gaius had done, adding in a deep, musical voice details that had been left out. Simeon explained how Marcus, the wise and good ruler of Khemia, had been warned in a dream that his homeland was about to be engulfed in a catastrophe. He ordered boats to be built, enough for all the souls on the island, and the people of Khemia had sailed from certain death to safety. He described their wonder and delight as they found themselves dis-embarking on a mysterious paradise. Everything seemed to be ready for them—a safe harbor and fields laden with fruit and grain. They lacked nothing. At Marcus's order the ships were torn apart, the wooden planks used to make the first shelters in their new land.

Simeon paused. "Soon after their arrival, Marcus declared that there was no need for weapons in this place of peace. Wars between neighboring tribes and peoples were a thing of the past, and so he ordered all the weap-ons they had brought with them—all the swords and bows and arrows—to be destroyed. Marcus put Thales in change of the destruction of the bows and arrows, and Brutus of the swords. Aedyn would be a place of peace and tranquility."

Simeon stopped speaking and closed his eyes. All was silent for a long moment while Julia sat on the edge of her seat. She knew the end of the story, and yet she longed to hear it told again. Finally she was driven to beg, "What happened next?"

Simeon's eyes opened. "Marcus was assassinated by Xenos, his most trusted lord. Within days he and his men had taken over the island, murdering anyone who stood in their way. You see, the swords had not been destroyed. They had been hidden, ready for this day. Xenos and his two treacherous aides, Thales and Brutus, declared themselves to be the rulers of this island. They gave themselves new names and new titles—you've seen this yourself," said Simeon, nodding to Julia. "The Jackal, the Leopard, and the Wolf: the Lords of Aedyn. Our fathers' fathers were given a choice: total obedience to the lords or death for them and their children. No mercy would be shown. They had no choice."

He put up his hands in a simple gesture of utter despair and hopelessness. Julia shivered.

"And that's the way it's been ever since?" she asked. Simeon nodded.

"For five hundred years, my lady," he said. "Five hundred years, until the memory of our good land and our good king has been all but stamped out. We kept it alive. Our parents told us the stories and we told them to our children—told them of Marcus, and the One who sent him the dream. We told them of the prophecy, and of the fair strangers who would come to fulfill it."

"But now," Helen broke in, "we may no longer even tell them our stories." There was an anger in her voice that seemed foreign to Julia—this was not the woman who had held her as she wept!

Simeon cleared his throat. "Some months ago," he said, "a few of our number escaped. The lords took our children—all our children. They're being held. We don't know where, we don't know for how long ..." His voice broke. "We only know that they'll be killed if we try to escape."

Julia felt herself go very, very pale.

"Your children?" she whispered. "So that's why it was so quiet in the streets ..." Her voice trailed off as she remembered the silent rows of houses outside the castle.

Simeon knelt in front of her, one knee pressed to the cold stone floor. He reached out and took Julia's chin in his hand, studying her face. She met his gaze, feeling once more the sharp sting of tears in her eyes.

"You've been called here, Julia," he said. "Called to help deliver our children and restore this land to the paradise the Lord of Hosts always intended it to be."

"The Lord ..." Julia repeated, confused.

"One greater than Marcus," said Simeon—the same words that Gaius had used in the garden. "It is a name we have been forbidden ever to mention on this island, on pain of death. It is a name that was daily on our lips in Khemia, and on this island until the death of

Marcus. This is the name by which we know our creator, the one who brought us into being. He is the one who warned Marcus of the coming destruction. He is the one who prepared this place for us. And he is the one whose memory the Lords of Aedyn wish to purge from this good land."

"Are you talking about God?" Julia asked bluntly. She'd never been much interested in God—he seemed too distant, too unreal—but here in Aedyn she felt intrigued. Enthralled, even.

Simeon smiled and stood, releasing her chin from his grasp. "We call him by the name he himself has asked us to use. He is the creator of all things, and the one who guides and cares for his people. And the one who will deliver us from our bondage."

They were interrupted by a slave, who burst in and slammed herself against the door. "The Lady Julia must leave immediately!" she hissed. "The guards are coming!"

"But I need to know ..."

"Leave now! Your life and ours depend on it!"

And Julia left, walking slowly and with dignity, as if she had no reason to hurry or be concerned about anything. She returned to her rooms unchallenged, her mind still racing, and came back to find her brother waiting for her.

He stood by a great window, looking out. There

was so much that she wanted to tell him, but she was not quite sure how much was safe to reveal. But the meeting with the slaves went out of her mind as she looked at her brother—there was something very wrong with him, she thought.

"What are you looking at, Peter? You seem worried about something."

He turned around and looked at her, his eyes wide. He shook his head mutely and pointed as Julia joined him at the window. Together they looked down at a group of guards far below, gathered round a barrel on one of the castle ramparts. As they watched, one of them lit a match.

Suddenly there was a loud explosion, and dense white smoke enveloped the scene. As it cleared, Julia and Peter could see that an entire section had been blown out of the castle rampart. Julia stared at the damaged stonework for some moments, shocked, and then turned to Peter in disbelief.

"Peter, please tell me that you didn't tell them how to make gunpowder!"

And there was nothing to say. Julia gripped the window ledge, her knuckles white. "Do you have any idea what you've done?" she hissed.

Peter whipped around. "I shared knowledge, just like you said. They're good people—they're men of science, of reason."

"And you're not concerned—not the slightest bit worried that these scientific lords might use their new weapon in a way that is not so nice and logical?"

Peter, reduced to a sullen, shameful silence, thought it best at this point that he avoid mentioning the part about being made a prince.

Beneath them guards rushed to the scene, hurrying to repair the damage to the building and tend to the injuries of their men. Peter turned to his sister, not able to look her straight in the eye.

"I don't know why you're so set against them. The slaves are slaves because they're deluded. Anaximander explained it all," he said in the haughty-older-brother voice which Julia most despised. "They're slaves because they have not ascended to a higher plane of reason."

Which was when Julia hit him.

She hadn't spent her growing-up years honing her skills at fisticuffs, but what she lacked in skill she made up for in rage. Peter didn't exactly go sprawling, but he stumbled back against the window ledge, his hand tight against the cheek she had struck. This was a Julia he had never encountered before.

"Look around you!" she hissed. "Science didn't bring us here. We were called—called by the Lord of Hosts, and we're supposed to fix this place. We're supposed to free the slaves."

"Lord of Hosts? Free the slaves? I told you,

they're practically barbarians," Peter said, stepping away
to avoid another fist if it came his way. "The lords have
it sorted."

"I've been hearing stories — the slaves' stories,"
said Julia, thinking quickly. She had been warned not to
repeat what she learned, and now she understood why:
Peter was not to be trusted. "The Jackal, Leopard, and
Wolf are the barbarians, and you've just handed them
their greatest weapon."

Peter began to look unaccountably smug. "Well,
not really," he said loftily. "They can make the powder
and it will go on exploding in their faces, but what they
really need are …"

"Guns," Julia finished. "You didn't tell them about
guns, did you?"

"Oh no," said Peter grandly. "I'm waiting until
they make me their pri …"

He wasn't able to stop the word from coming
out in time. Julia stared at him incredulously, and his
smug expression faded.

"Peter, you are impossible," she said, and stalked
out of the chamber.

Peter stayed at the window long after Julia had left for her own rooms, watching the chaos below. Guards and slaves rushed back and forth, scurrying to clear away the rubble that had once been ornate stonework. As he watched, the Wolf came into view.

He was there to survey the damage, Peter realized. He exchanged a few quick words with the captain of the guards and then he stalked around looking poisonous, his voluminous robes sweeping over the dust and debris.

His head came up suddenly and he looked straight at Peter, high up at the window. His face was obscured as usual beneath the mask, but Peter could sense the anger in his stare. There was something cold in it—something primal. Something that sought revenge.

It was too late to duck away and avoid being seen. Fear flooded into Peter, and for the first time he felt the power of the Wolf's presence—the power that had kept innocent people in chains for centuries. His limbs went numb under the anger of that silent stare, but with the force of overwhelming willpower he told himself to keep calm. And then, as he watched, the Wolf held up his arm and pointed at Peter, deliberately and accusingly. Peter felt a shiver go down his spine: he had given the lords a weapon but not shown them how to use it, and he would have to pay the price. He put his hands in his pockets and turned away from the window, trying with all his might to look like a prince.

Late that afternoon Peter and Julia were summoned to the Great Hall. They both knew what could happen, but death is not a simple thing to face in one's youth. And so they went into the hall with confidence, standing as tall as their father when he stood at the helm of one of his ships, facing the open ocean before him.

The three lords sat on their thrones, their every movement exaggerated by those voluminous robes. Their masks were, if it was possible, more stoic, more opaque than ever before. Julia felt an unaccustomed chill go through her bones as she walked towards them.

The Wolf—Xenos, she remembered from Simeon's story—spoke first. He spoke simply and to the point, his voice entirely without emotion. He sounded, thought Julia, almost as if he were bored.

"For planting false information under the guise of friendship and deliberately sabotaging an experiment performed in the name of science, Peter and Julia, emissaries of Albion across the sea, you are sentenced to death by hanging at first light."

And that was all there was. He raised a hand and dropped it in a dismissive gesture, and before Peter or Julia could say a word the guards had taken hold of them, twisting their hands tight behind their backs and dragging them back out of the Hall.

Julia tried without a great deal of success to shake them off, and then, as the harsh reality of their situation dawned on her, she went absolutely still. She stared, wide-eyed and mute, as Peter cried out.

"A word in private, my lords!"

The Jackal, the Leopard, and the Wolf looked up at him—in shock, perhaps, for when had a prisoner ever dared to question them? The Wolf nodded and beckoned him forward. The guard holding Peter loosened his grip, and Peter shook him off as he approached the thrones.

As he spoke softly to the three lords Julia strained to hear what was being said, but could make out only snatches of the conversation. But the words she could hear sent her heart plummeting into her stomach.

" … show you how to make a cannon … must be allowed to go free …"

Peter then stepped backwards, allowing the lords to consult among themselves.

If he had happened to look at Julia just then he might have seen the most curious mix of emotions on her face: distrust, confusion, fear, and anger—anger above all. But he kept his eyes carefully focused on the polished tile of the ground beneath his feet.

After a few moments the Wolf stood, addressing

the guards. "Take the lady Julia to the Death Cage. Lord Peter will live."

Julia remembered then what had happened in the meadow, when the three horsemen were reduced to whimpers of pain at her screams. She opened her mouth with a vague idea of doing the same—of hurting the guards, hurting the lords, hurting Peter—but all that came out were sobs.

She shivered with cold and fear as she was dragged from the Hall, sobbing for anyone—Helen, Alyce, Simeon—anyone who would make this all right again. And so, with her eyes shut tight against the horrors of Aedyn, she didn't see her brother finally looking at her, staring after her captors in stark horror.

CHAPTER

10

Peter watched the door close with a dull, final thud, and felt for perhaps the first time in his life that he was utterly alone.

"Now, Peter," came the hissing voice of the Wolf, "perhaps you would be so good as to share your secrets?"

"Show us how to harness your gunpowder," rasped the Leopard. Peter made a sound rather like a gulp and stepped forward. This was not at all what he had intended—but what else was there to do? How else could he save his sister? If he gave them the diagram of a cannon he would save Julia by making the Jackal, the Leopard, and the Wolf invincible. Was the cost too high?

Peter decided he must get a grip of himself. His own life and that of his sister were at stake. He simply could not afford to make any more mistakes. He stepped forward and looked directly at the Wolf. Behind that mask, he told himself, was an ordinary human being. There was nothing to fear from a mask.

"My lord, I gave you the secret of gunpowder. But this is of little use without the weapon to direct the blast over great distances. We call these weapons cannons. I am prepared to tell you how to make one, but there are conditions."

The Leopard laughed—a cold, gravelly laugh that held no trace of joy. "You are in no position to negotiate. We have ways of making you tell us what we need to know."

Peter squared his shoulders and tried to look brave. "I will tell you nothing that I have not agreed to, my lords. Of that you can be certain. I am offering to give you this information on certain conditions."

Again that gasping laugh from the Leopard, but the Wolf intervened, motioning the others to silence.

"We would like to hear your conditions, Lord Peter. Pray tell us."

"Freedom for the lady Julia and myself. Freedom … and a boat, so that we might return to our own land." A boat wouldn't do them much good, he knew. Somehow they had to get back to that garden and make the pond become a portal back to Oxford. But freedom had to come first.

The Wolf nodded slowly, his eyes fixed on Peter. "Rebellion against the state is a capital crime. The penalty is severe and immediate. Traitors must die. You know that. Normally, we would ..."

Peter's heart leapt at the word "normally." Surely this meant that they were about to make an exception in his case?

"Normally, we would insist on immediate execution. But if you serve us in this way, we will allow you and your companion to leave Aedyn. You will supervise the construction and testing of this weapon, and you will have your freedom if the test is successful. If it is not, you will die. Is that clear?"

Peter gulped again. This was getting out of control. But what other option did he have?

"That is very satisfactory, my lord. I have your word on this?"

"You have the word of the Wolf." The lord stood and reached out a pale hand to Peter, who took it in his. "Now you will return to your apartment. You will remain there under guard while you show us how to build this cannon of which you speak so highly."

At a nod of his head the guards turned on their heels and dragged Peter away from the Great Hall and back to his chambers. He heard the ominous click of the lock as the door was closed behind him. He was alone. He looked out of the windows of his apartment. The darkening night matched his mood as one thought whirled over and over through his mind: what reason did the lords have to keep him and Julia alive if the cannon worked?

Julia had been thrown into a wooden cage just outside the castle grounds, the door locked behind her. Two guards patrolled outside. As the sun left the sky in a burst of oranges and pinks Julia closed her eyes and wept, enveloped by the deep gloom of hopelessness. There was nothing that she could do or say to make things better. Her fate lay beyond her control. She watched the guards marching up and down with a growing sense of despair. Was there any way to escape?

Unaccountably, her mother sprang to her mind. Not her mother as she had been in the end, lying weak and pale in bed, unable to eat, unable to speak, unable to hold her own children. No, she thought of her mother as she had been in the years before. Strong and tall—just as tall as her husband, and with all of his fire and bravery. She had been, Julia thought, a great woman. She would have known what to do. She would have known how to help the slaves and how to get home. She would have found a way out of this cage.

Help would certainly not come from her brother. Peter had abandoned and betrayed her, taken in by the dark lords of Aedyn and his silly need to impress, to be on top. She rested her chin on her knees and looked up at the night sky. The stars were winking into place in the purple velvet heavens. And then she remembered Gaius and Simeon, and how they had spoken of the One who was greater than Marcus. Surely this was the moment to call on him. So there and then, on that dark, cold night, Julia asked the Lord of Hosts to be at her side. To stand by her, even in this darkest hour. And to help her set his people free. Then, exhausted, she fell asleep on the uncomfortable floor of the cage.

Something woke her some hours later—she could never be sure how many. It was still night, and the guards were still patrolling. But something was different—some hint of intrigue was in the air. Julia stayed still, rooted to the spot in apprehension. In the moonlight she could just make out a small group of shadowy figures coming soundlessly toward her—was she to be executed immediately? She wanted to scream, wanted to cry out for help, but what good could that do? There was no escape from the Death Cage.

As the figures came closer Julia could distinguish four of them. The two smallest seemed to lurk behind in the background—perhaps to prevent any escape for the doomed prisoner. The other two were running towards the Death Cage, silently but swiftly. They reached the guards, who had not seen or heard them coming.

In the darkness Julia could not be quite sure what was happening, but she could see a scuffle between the two figures and the men guarding the cage. The strangers had the element of surprise on their side but the guards were quick and well-trained, and for a moment it looked as if they might gain the upper hand. But finally the guards were overpowered, and the two figures in the background approached to help tie and gag them. Not a word was spoken. It was as if the whole operation had been well planned in advance. Julia watched in astonishment as one of the raiders extracted a set of keys from one of the guards and opened the door. The stranger made quick work of the ropes that bound Julia's hands and helped her roughly to her feet. "Who are you?" she hissed, rubbing her wrists where the ropes had cut into her skin.

"I am Lukas," the stranger said briefly. "Gaius sent me from the forest. You'll be safe with us. Come." The two trussed guards were dragged into the Death Cage and the doors locked. Lukas hid the keys within his robes as Julia looked, for the first time, at the other figures.

"Alyce—and Helen!" she breathed. The younger woman grinned and Helen caught Julia into a hard embrace. "How—how did you …"

"There is no time for stories," said the fourth figure, a man whom Julia did not recognize. "We ride."

Lukas guided Julia into the darkness of the trees, where five horses stood tethered and waiting. A few moments later, just as dawn was beginning to touch the sky, they galloped off toward the dark forest of the west.

CHAPTER

11

The Lords of Aedyn looked up with irritation as a guard knocked at the door and opened it to admit Anaximander. The Jackal sighed deeply, annoyed at the intrusion. They had been discussing their plans over breakfast for the new weapon which Peter had agreed to design for them.

Anaximander was robed in his ceremonial best and had planned to deliver a great deal of flowery speeches along with his news. But something he saw in the Wolf's posture—something in the dead coldness of the eyes behind that mask—indicated that this might not have been the wisest approach. And so he said, quite simply and without apology, "My Lord, the prisoner has escaped."

An awful silence fell upon the room. The Wolf stood, and the eyes behind the mask were no longer cold but full of fire. But the Leopard spoke instead. "You will interrogate the guards who permitted her escape. We need to know if they had help from inside the castle."

Anaximander nodded. "It is almost certain that she was freed by renegade slaves—the same who got away from the working party some months ago, overpowering their guards."

"Another failure on your part," said the Wolf in that strange, emotionless voice. "Go. Find out what happened—and remember that the fair stranger must know nothing of what has transpired. We shall discuss your future on your return."

The Lord Chamberlain paused for an imperceptible moment, then bowed low to the lords, turned on his heel, and left the Hall. He walked as one already condemned. Unless he sorted this out very quickly, he would be dead within days. The Lords of Aedyn tolerated no failure on the part of their servants.

Knowing he would need his rest, Peter had forced himself to go to bed. But he'd slept poorly and rose with the first light of dawn. With nothing to do, he paced up and down inside his apartment, hungry, miserable, and more convinced with each passing moment that he had made a terrible mistake. The Lords of Aedyn were evil, but that did not make them fools. He had been mad to think that they would allow Julia to go free simply because he told them how to make a cannon! And of course they would want to make sure it worked before releasing her. He should have seen that coming.

Peter sighed and ran a hand roughly through his hair. What a mess! He racked his mind again, trying to work out whether there was anything that could still be done to turn the situation around. But what could he do? His apartment was now kept locked from the outside, and he could not leave the room—much less the castle—without the permission of the Lords of Aedyn. He was under house arrest, and there was nothing left to do. He sat down on the bed, his head in his hands. If only he could think of something clever that would get them all out of this mess! Some drastic escape, and a heroic rescue for Julia …

The door swung open. The captain of the guards entered, accompanied by two of his men. His face was grim, and he wasted no words. "You will come with me to the Great Hall to show us the construction of your cannon." A slave entered the room behind him, carrying a tray with a simple meal. "Eat," said the captain. "You have five minutes. I shall be waiting outside for you." He and his men left the room, locking its great door behind them.

Peter drank deeply from the cup and tore off a

piece of bread. His last meal, he thought grimly. He was just about to bite into the bread when he noticed that something was wrong. There was a piece of paper rolled up inside it.

Looking around to make sure he was not being watched, Peter unrolled the paper, his eyes going wide at the message written within.

"J escaped. Safe in forest. Destroy this message."

Peter read it again, making sure his eyes weren't playing tricks on him. Julia was safe—safe in spite of all his stupid blunders. He wondered who could have sent the message—maybe one of the slaves of whom Julia had seemed so fond? There was no way that the Lords of Aedyn would tell him about this. They wanted him to think he was at their mercy. But if this message was true, they no longer had any way of controlling him.

Hurriedly Peter placed the rest of the bread in his mouth and began to chew. There were no more messages. Finally, he crumpled up the paper up into a little ball and swallowed it, grimacing. He knocked on his door for the guards to let him out, and as he left the apartment a plan began to form in his mind just as a smile began to form on his lips.

"Are you ready?" asked the captain.

"Yes, I'm ready," said Peter.

CHAPTER

12

Julia and her companions galloped into the forest of the west, the sun slowly rising behind them and bathing them in its red glow. Lukas reined in his steed, checking that his companions were safe and they were not being pursued. Once deep in the forest they would be safe. None but those who dwelt in the wood itself knew its hidden paths and trails. Outsiders would be lost within moments, enveloped in its green wilderness without any means of finding their bearings. In some parts of the forest the light of the sun never penetrated the dense canopy of leaves, and Lukas and his followers had made their base in the darkest and most impenetrable region. Here they would be well hidden.

As the rising sun was just beginning to burn the mist off the ground they entered the forest. Julia looked around her. She had been here before but she knew no landmarks to help her find her way. She was grateful for those riding with her, for she was not a strong rider and could not have directed her horse alone.

But the sure-footed horses seemed to know where they were going. They needed no guidance, and after an hour's ride they came to a halt in a clearing. Everyone dismounted, relieved to stretch their legs after the ride. Lukas gathered them together and pointed towards some logs piled at one edge of the open space.

"We will rest here for a few moments. The horses will no longer accompany us. They have done their job, and done it well." He bowed to the five horses, and they lowered their heads briefly in return before cantering off down a trail that Julia had failed to notice. She wanted to know where the horses were going—she had so many questions that she didn't really know where to begin. How had Helen and Alyce escaped the palace? Where was she being taken? But this, she suspected, was not the right time to ask questions. This was a time for action, not conversation.

Julia sat down on a log. A dark green tunic, just her size, was draped over its branches. She looked around and noticed that the others were already shedding their black robes and changing into the tunics. Camouflage. The robes were being buried in a shallow hole back in the trees: they would leave no evidence.

She changed quickly, discarding the heavy bro-
cades of the castle, and turned to continue the journey.
Lukas nodded approvingly and beckoned towards another trail leading from the clearing into the denser forest.

"This is the road down which we must travel. We
are nearly at our journey's end, but we must be quiet.
Noises travel, even in the forest. They say that the trees
have ears, and no one can know that we have traveled
this path. So keep quiet, and follow me."

The five travelers moved off down the trail,
Lukas leading and his comrade bringing up the rear.

It was not much further before they reached
their destination. Julia had no doubt where it was. They
were back at the secret garden she and Peter had discov-
ered on their first day on Aedyn. But she tried hard not
to think of Peter—it would only make her angry. And
anyway, she was sure she would have enough to think
about without worrying about his treachery.

The five travelers entered the garden. The monk
Gaius rose to meet them, greeting Julia and embracing
the four others. "You have done well," he said to them.

Gaius beckoned to them to join him at a table
that had appeared near to the throne, covered with
fresh bread and luscious fruits. He smiled at his visitors.

"We can talk safely now. We are too deep in the
forest for any lackeys of the dark lords to find us. There
are eagles posted throughout this region, and they will

know what to do if strangers approach. We will have plenty of warning." He turned to Helen and Alyce, nodding at them. "It is many years since you have been in this garden, is it not?"

Alyce smiled up at Lukas. "Not since I was a child, and taken to serve in the castle," she said. "I never thought this day would come."

"We'll help the others escape soon," Lukas said gently, touching her arm. "We would have tonight, had we more horses …"

Helen was looking around, taking in the scene. "Gaius, it's ruined! What happened to the garden? To the fountain? To everything!"

The monk nodded, his expression grim.

"It is as you say. The garden mirrors the condition of Aedyn itself, and it is in a sad state of ruin and decay. But when Aedyn is renewed, this garden will once more become the place Marcus knew. Even the garden you remember cannot compare to that! And that day is to hand." His gaze shifted to Julia, who tried all of a sudden to look very small. "The fair strangers have come," he said softly, "and the Lord of Hosts will visit and restore his people. He has seen our suffering at the hands of our oppressors, and the time has come. He has raised up a deliverer who will break the power of the dark lords."

Julia blushed, not precisely sure what to say. How could she save anyone or anything? Peter always used to tease her for being clumsy and silly—and how could a girl of thirteen deliver a nation from such evil? But someone had to do it. Maybe she had yet to discover herself. It all seemed so—well, so improbable. But how could she walk away when the need was so great?

Gaius nodded at Julia, seeming to read her thoughts. "No one is ever ready for the world to turn upside down, dear one. And so we have brought you here to prepare yourself for what must come."

What must come ... the man seemed to speak exclusively in riddles, Julia thought. In anyone else, this would have been intensely irritating. Gaius smiled at her and continued.

"You will go deep into the forest. During that time, you will discover whether you really are the deliverer that we have been awaiting. You will remain there for a time and then return here, to this garden. It is tomorrow that we mark the Great Remembrance."

"The Great ... what?" repeated Julia. "Is that what you told me about before, when everyone comes to tell stories?"

Helen stepped forward. Her eyes were bright, and for the first time Julia caught a glimpse of the joyful young woman that, in a different time and place, she might have been. She spoke in a voice that was serene, and somehow far away.

"We came out of a distant land, Lady Julia, and

were led over the seas to this island. It would be a new beginning for us as a people. We would be the good Lord's
people in a good land. When our ancestors arrived in
Aedyn, Marcus told them that they were to mark their
safe arrival in the new paradise. Every year, the story of
the journey across the sea to this island would be told
again. We will never forget this moment in our history,
nor the faithfulness of the One who brought us here.
Marcus was the first to tell that story, in the Great Hall of
the Citadel of the Lord of Hosts. It is a solemn reminder
of our past. Our identity as a people is so closely inter-
twined with this event that we must never forget it. The
dark lords think that they have suppressed this event
by preventing it from happening in the castle—they
know that the surest way to destroy a people is to erase
the memory of their past. But this garden was built as
a way of remembering the past and looking forward to
the future." She smiled at the monk. "Gaius is our story
keeper, the one who guards our history. We come and
remember, and wait for the deliverer." And then, looking at Gaius, her eyes went dark. "Of course, there are
not many who can come to remember. So many of the
faithful are enslaved in the castle ..." Her voice trailed
off, and Gaius took up the story.

   "We need you here for the Great Remembrance,
Lady Julia. If you believe that the Lord of Hosts has
called you to deliver us from the dark lords, then you

will be acclaimed as our deliverer. And then you must find the answers to the great question of Aedyn. Only then can we hope to break free from the dark power of the lords."

Julia was absolutely baffled.

"Question? What—what question? I don't know this place well enough to …" Gaius hushed her.

"Julia, we need to know why Marcus' most trusted lords betrayed our paradise. We need to know how such evil could arise in this place. Unless we can find the root of the evil, we shall never be able to restore this paradise to what it was meant to be. We must destroy the source of this evil before it can contaminate others." He smiled at her expression—a look of intense concentration and utter confusion, and took her hands between his. "If you are indeed the deliverer, you will not struggle on your own. The Lord of Hosts will be with you. He will guide you and give you new power as you seek answers."

"I will do my best, Gaius."

"I know you will." He squeezed her hands as his eyes smiled at her. "You will leave this garden in two hours and go deeper into the forest, but now you must rest. You will need all your strength for what lies ahead."

CHAPTER

13

Peter, as he accompanied the captain of the guard to the Great Hall, was feeling immensely pleased with himself. Now that Julia had escaped, he thought, he could give the lords a faulty design for their cannon without worrying about her safety. He had recalled something from one of his grandfather's long talks—lectures, more like—about Lord Nelson's naval strategies at the Battle of Trafalgar. If cannons were not made properly they exploded, killing those who loaded and fired them.

His idea was simple—simple but brilliant, he told himself. He would get the lords to make a clay cannon and clay cannonballs. Clay could never withstand the force of an explosion. The weapon that the Lords of Aedyn hoped to use against their enemies would destroy their own guards instead.

There was, of course, the simple matter of his own escape, but as they approached the Hall he put it out of his mind. All would be well. He was sure of it.

All three lords were waiting. One of them gestured to a table that had been set up with paper and ink and Peter, understanding, made a hasty but complete sketch of a cannon. Finishing, he brought it to the lords.

"You put the gunpowder all the way down here," he said, pointing. "And the cannonball—those are the clay balls I told you about—is placed on top of it. Then the gunpowder is ignited through this little opening here. It explodes and propels the cannonball into the distance."

"And how far does it travel?" asked the Jackal.

"It all depends, my lord," Peter replied. "That's part of the testing process. But it will go far indeed—farther than an arrow."

"But surely the cannon itself will explode? How could clay withstand the pressure?"

"The barrel of the cannon is very thick, and the cannonball does not stay inside for long," Peter said self-assuredly. "The full force of the explosion will propel the cannonball forward, not shatter the cannon barrel."

"I do hope you're right," said the Wolf, speaking for the first time. "If not, you can expect to die a particularly unpleasant death. You!" He addressed a swarthy

man who was standing back in the shadows—the potter, and most likely another slave, Peter thought. "Can
this be made?" The Wolf took hold of Peter's design and
shook it at the man. The potter nodded mutely and gave
a grunt that must have been assent, for the lords seemed
to relax.

"Until tomorrow, then," said the Wolf, and swept
his arm in a gesture of dismissal.

Peter returned to his rooms, locked in with a
guard stationed outside the doorway. He paced back
and forth in front of the windows, no longer able to
push out of his mind the question of his escape. Surely,
surely there had to be a way to get out of all this. A way
to get away from the castle and find Julia and get home
to Oxford!

It was just then, as he looked out over the castle
ramparts, that the shadow of an idea slipped into his
mind. He walked up and down more heavily, mulling it
over. It would depend ninety percent upon careful plan-
ning and ten percent on blind luck, and Peter knew that
one cannot plan to be lucky. But the risk was still worth
taking. He thought furiously. The plan had so many
loose ends, but it was the only one he had. It just had to
work. Otherwise, he would die a quick death when the
cannon exploded ... or a slow one when the Lords of
Aedyn caught him afterwards.

As Peter paced the room Julia was setting off into the dark depths of the forest.

"How will I know where I am meant to be going?" she asked Gaius, gripping the new walking stick Lukas had cut for her.

"An eagle will go ahead of you, and he will guide you to the place of testing. Look up on that tree, to the right. No, just there. Do you see him? Watch him carefully. When you have arrived at the right place, he will land close beside you." Gaius put his hands on Julia's shoulders and squeezed them gently, just as her father had done when she was small. "Now go! And may the Lord of Hosts be with you!"

There was a fluttering noise from the tree as the eagle launched himself into the air and began to soar upwards, circling. Julia followed him along a narrow path which seemed to lead nowhere.

It was late morning, but as she followed the eagle deeper and deeper into the forest it seemed that dusk had begun to fall. She found herself deep in the shadowy, wild forest, and had it not been for the dark outline of the eagle above her she would have been lost in moments. Immense, gloomy trees with huge twisted roots soared up to an invisible yet darkening sky far beyond. The tangled maze of leaves and branches were like a thick wall, blotting out what little remained of the sunlight.

She had no idea what creatures might lurk in the darkness beyond the safety of the path, or what wild beasts might live on the island. But she kept her eyes on the eagle, and suddenly the path opened up into a grassy clearing. The eagle waited in the middle of it, cocking its head at her almost inquisitively. Then he bowed—and if you have ever seen an eagle bow, you will know that it was a very strange sight indeed—and flew into the gathering night. Within moments, he had disappeared from view.

Julia watched him depart—her one link with the familiar. How she wished that she could mount up with the wings of an eagle, instead of being bound to this island and the great unknown!

Alone in the night, this unaccustomed midday darkness, there was nothing to do but make herself comfortable and wait for whatever this test might be. She stretched out beneath a thick-branched pine at the edge of the clearing and, still exhausted from her night in the Death Cage and the hard ride after it, waited for sleep to come.

But something else came first.

In front of her eyes the tall grasses between the trees parted, revealing what lay within. A man stepped out from between the trees and held out his hand. "Greetings," he said with a smile.

CHAPTER

14

He wore the dark robes of a slave, but the massive hood was down around his shoulders. His silver hair and hard eyes were all too familiar. Simeon. She hadn't expected to see him here—he was still a slave in the castle, wasn't he? But stranger things had already happened in Aedyn, and so she started forward with a smile. Simeon opened his arms in an embrace.

"What are you doing here?" she asked, her eyes bright. Simeon dipped his head in a gesture that was almost a bow.

"I bear greetings to the Deliverer of Aedyn!"

Julia smiled shyly. The name sounded grander every time she heard it—the Deliverer. The Deliverer.

"But how did you get out of the castle?" she

asked. "I thought you were all trapped there …"

"I have my ways," he answered. "I come from your friends. Friends who recognize your strength and power and wisdom. Friends who want to help you to use it!"

Strength. Power. Wisdom. She straightened her back and smiled, wishing in spite of herself that Peter could hear what Simeon was saying. "Go on," she said.

"My lady, Gaius has told you that you were called here to serve others. But why not serve yourself instead? You have no rival in this island. Why not claim it for your own? Why give power to another when you could have that power yourself? You could be," he said quietly, "the supreme ruler. My friends and I would be your slaves. We would count it a great honor to serve one such as you."

And Julia's imagination was set on fire. Every person and animal on this island bowing down to her—their adoring cries ringing in her ears. She was captivated.

"And what must I do to become the supreme ruler of this world?"

Simeon smiled. "Nothing, my lady, nothing. We will do everything for you. All you need do is speak when we tell you to. We will tell you what to say."

Julia was overwhelmed with images of luxury, delight, and power. But then she looked at Simeon —looked at his eyes—and other images began to intrude. She saw a bird beating itself against the bars of a golden cage, trying with all its strength to escape. That was what this was all about. Trickery and temptation. She could follow Simeon—if this was indeed Simeon—and become merely a figurehead for the dark forces that still enslaved the island.

Her eyes snapped back into focus, and she remembered who she was and what she was meant to do. A new strength flooded through her, and she spoke in a voice that she hardly recognized as her own. "I am not the fool you think, Simeon. Leave me."

The man before her made an almost inhuman snarl before slinking back into the night.

Julia looked after him long after he had vanished into the forest. She was breathing heavily, taking in great gulps of air as she watched the place where he had been. And finally she returned to her place beneath the pine, longing for rest.

She could not say how long she had slept when she was roused by a soft noise, somehow set apart from the normal din of the woods. As she listened, all senses alert, she heard the soft beating of wings in the night air. She sat bolt upright, her eyes straining into the darkness to see what was coming.

It was the eagle—the same who had brought her to this place. She was silent, suspicious as it landed close by her and bowed low.

"Hail, Lady Julia. I come from Gaius, and I bring you new instructions."

"And what are these orders?"

"You are in great danger," said the eagle with something like a smile. "The Lords of Aedyn are coming for you. I am to lead you to a hiding place. You will be safe there, and among friends."

"And what does Gaius want me to do while I wait there?" she asked, unwilling to trust the eagle, no matter how convincing his words. But it came up close to her and rubbed its face against her skirts, roughly but not harshly. Julia was suddenly reminded of Scamp, her grandparents' tabby cat back home in Oxford, and she reached down to stroke the smooth feathers on the eagle's head.

"He and the rebels will fight," the eagle spoke, its voice low. "You are too precious to risk your life in battle, my lady. The people need to see you victorious."

Safety ... safety and friends. What could be sweeter? Julia began to nod, and then stopped. She had not been called from another world to remain safe. She had been called to lead.

Julia stared at the animal. Outwardly he was noble and dignified, yet she knew in her heart of hearts that inwardly he was trying to lure her into a trap. It was not reasoned thinking that brought her to this conclusion, for she knew the eagle to be her guide. It was something deeper than reason, some kind of wisdom that seemed to be taking her over and directing her judgments. She would be taken to a place of "safety" where she would be assassinated. Or captured, and taken back in chains to the Lords of Aedyn. No, she would not trust him.

"Begone, Eagle," she said. "Go back to your masters. I will not suffer your presence here." The bird hissed at her, hatred pouring out of his molten eyes.

"You fool! You will die for this."

"No," she said quietly. "You are the one who will die. Those who sent you do not tolerate failure." And with another hiss, the eagle beat his wings and lifted himself into the stillness.

Julia returned to the pine once more, determined to stay awake and await whatever might come next. But sleep overtook her, and when she woke again the sun was just touching the sky with the easy grace of dawn. She remembered how she had seen it the day before, riding away into a forest, and for a moment she wondered about Peter—wondered if he was safe and well, in spite of all he had done to her. And then she put him out of her mind because there was a more pressing matter at hand: breakfast.

She clutched at her stomach and looked about for the eagle—the true eagle, not the imposter of the night. Surely he would take her back to the garden, and Gaius would conjure more of his breads and fruit for her. Surely the testing was over and it was safe to return!

And then came a rustling noise in the forest to her left. Instantly she was on alert. As she looked around, every muscle tense, the grasses parted to reveal a tall, slender woman whose gentle eyes were most familiar.

Julia let out a gasp and then a cry, lurching forward into her mother's waiting arms. And if you have ever longed for someone—longed with your whole being to be with that person—you will be able to imagine how sweet the reunion was.

There was a great deal of weeping and hugging, and even when Julia stepped back she could hardly believe it. Her mother—her mother who had died. But stranger things could happen in Aedyn, couldn't they? Even Gaius could live here, century after century, after he had died on Earth. And so she didn't waste any breath asking how her mother could be there, but just drank in the sight of her.

"Let me look at you." Her mother held Julia at arm's length, a smile playing around the corners of her mouth. "My beautiful girl ... my girl. You'll come with me, won't you?"

"Come where?" she asked. Her mother gestured her head back the way she had come.

"I've made a place for us, darling. A place we can be together—somewhere safe where you can rest. You don't have to be a hero anymore." Julia let out a gaspy little sob and collapsed against her mother, who put her arm around her waist and started to lead her out of the clearing.

She spoke softly while they walked—reassuring words of such peace and comfort that Julia almost wept with the relief of it. No more fighting. No more trying to be brave.

"We'll stay there together," her mother was saying. "It's a cozy little house. I built a room for you— all for you. And we won't have to miss each other any more, because it will just be us. You and me. Peter won't come to bother us; it will just be us, darling."

And Julia stopped dead in her tracks.

"Not Peter?"

"Of course not, darling," her mother purred. "Peter hurt you, didn't he? Peter betrayed you."

"How do you know that?" Julia's eyes narrowed, suddenly suspicious.

"I know everything, dearest," her mother said with a laugh, but Julia stepped back, pained. This wasn't her mother—couldn't be her mother. Her mother would never speak a word against either of her children. And so she couldn't follow this—this apparition, no matter how safe it felt. The price would be high. Too high.

The woman watched Julia intently. But then the truth became clear: Julia was no child. Instead, her eyes meeting the steely gaze of one who had faced her weaknesses and triumphed over them. And so she nodded, turned, and was gone.

Julia stared after her, tears once more stinging her eyes, and watched, moments later, as the eagle—the true eagle—circled the clearing, leading her on a path to the north. Grateful, exhausted, Julia followed.

She walked as the sun rose, filtering through the rich foliage canopy above them. The path gradually became broader, and fluctuating patterns of light shimmered on the forest floor. Beams of light were caught in the rising mist from a nearby stream. The air became warmer and was gradually filled with the soft whooping and chirruping of waking birds and insects. It was, she realized, the first time she had heard the noises of natural animals in all the time she had spent in the forest. Something had changed.

Far above the eagle soared, rising with the warm air and diving down again to ensure he had not lost sight of his charge. Ahead, he caught the glint of sunlight reflected off the shimmering blue surface of the pool he was seeking. He fluttered down to the forest beneath him, perching on a branch high above the pathway. He watched as Julia made her way along the path towards him, and then, with two powerful thrusts of his wings, dived down to land by the side of a pool.

She sat down by the edge. It was clearly not a natural formation. The pool was perfectly round, surrounded by a low, carefully crafted stone wall. Its water was bright blue. To her right there was a small hill covered with trees. Down its side shimmered a small stream which babbled its way to the pool. *There must be a spring there*, she thought to herself. She touched it with her finger, then put her finger to her mouth. The water was cool and refreshing.

She lay down on the ground, stretched out in the soft sunlight, plunged her hands into the water and drank. Julia watched in pleasure as the surface of the water reflected the trees above, light flashing from time to time as the leaves moved in the gentle breeze.

Slowly, unnoticed, a figure detached itself from the green wilderness. He approached the pool slowly and sat down nearby. He watched Julia drink for a few moments, then spoke.

"Good morning, fair one."

Julia sat up abruptly, startled to find that she was not alone. But seeing who it was, she relaxed.

"Greetings, Gaius. It is good to see you."

"And you." He smiled broadly, his eyes twinkling. "You have done well. You have confronted ambition, deceit, and desire, and triumphed over all. And I think you have conquered self-love as well. Look into the pool. What do you see?"

Julia returned to the pool, lay down, and looked once more.

"I see the leaves of the trees and the sky beyond."

"Is there anything else?"

"Nothing," she replied, confused.

"Look again," urged the monk. "Is there anything missing?"

Julia peered back into the waters and let out a gasping breath. "I cannot see myself!"

The monk's eyes twinkled all the brighter. "That is the answer I hoped for. You have set love for yourself behind you, and in its place you will serve others.

Come." He stood and held out a hand. "My people are waiting for you to lead them. We must go now, and prepare for the Great Remembrance!"

He clapped his hands and the eagle flew upwards, no longer needed. Gaius would guide them back to the garden.

Onward they marched, heading towards the ruined garden and the Great Remembrance. And as they walked both pondered the same thought: Tonight, we shall do more than remember the past. We shall change the future!

CHAPTER

15

It was time to test the cannon. Peter had risen early, wanting to plan for the day ahead and figure out exactly how he was going to throw the sinister Lords of Aedyn into chaos. By the time the slave entered with a tray holding a meagre breakfast, he still wasn't sure his plan would work. So much still depended on luck.

He munched thoughtfully on the piece of stale bread that composed his breakfast as he reviewed his options. They seemed no clearer, and there were no more messages concealed in the bread. He would just have to hope for the best. "When in doubt, improvise!" he thought. (That was the slogan of his drama teacher at school. It had led to some very creative versions of Shakespeare's *Hamlet*.)

Two guards arrived to escort him to the testing ground, which had been prepared just outside the main castle walls. Nobody wanted to risk another explosion within the castle grounds. In any case, the Lords of Aedyn wanted to maintain secrecy about the new weapon that they hoped to add to their armoury. The cannon would be fired well away from places where people might see it.

Peter looked around him, feeling the heat of the sun on his neck. He noted that some guards had assembled on a raised rocky platform of land outside one of the main gates. They were gathered around the clay cannon, which they had mounted on a wooden trestle. Ahead of them lay the great forest, stretching far into the distance. The cannon pointed towards the wood. Unless the cannonball travelled a very great distance, they would be able to see where it hit the ground ahead of them.

The guards were kicking two slaves who had been instructed to secure the cannon on the rock platform. An open canvas sack of gunpowder was placed beside the cannon along with two cannon balls. Some horses loitered nearby, tearing at the long grass that grew alongside the rocks — stallions of the Jackal, the Leopard, and the Wolf, and a fourth for the captain of the guard.

The captain marched towards Peter.

"Show us how to load this infernal device. And no tricks. Clear?"

"Clear," muttered Peter as he poured gunpowder into the barrel and carefully lowered a cannonball on top of it. He checked that the touch hole was filled with gunpowder, placed a piece of wadding on top, and stood back from the weapon.

"It's ready."

It was ready … and as soon as fire hit the gunpowder everything would explode in his face. He took a deep breath. "Captain, those horses will bolt when they hear the noise of the explosion. They might injure themselves. Can you get someone to lead them back a bit and hold them?"

The captain grunted his assent and shouted toward the slaves.

"You there! Take the lords' horses over there against that wall. And don't dare let go of them. They're far more valuable than you are." He turned back to Peter. "Now tell us what to do, and what to look for."

Peter looked at the rock platform. The cannon was in its center, about twenty paces from the horses against the wall. A number of guards in addition to the captain were milling about, all fascinated by this new piece of technology, and by its side was an open canvas bag of gunpowder. The Jackal, the Leopard, and the Wolf stood on a platform some distance away, surveying the scene before them. It was perfect.

"The cannon will fire one of these balls a distance

over there, towards the forest," Peter said, pointing. "I want you and your men to watch carefully for signs of impact. Then we need to go to where the cannonball has landed, and work out how far it has travelled. That will help us calibrate the weapon. Is that clear?" Peter was trying very, very hard to sound like his father, trying to sound commanding and authoritative.

"Perfectly. You four! Stand over there. Keep your eyes peeled straight ahead of you. Don't look round! I don't want you missing this ball when it hits the ground. Now"—he turned back to Peter, who was intent on the slaves moving the horses. "What else?"

"Well," he said, trying to look once more like an emissary of Albion, "I ought to have the privilege of firing the weapon. After all, I designed it. I'll just need a match." He looked over his shoulder expectantly.

Peter was taking a gamble and it paid off. The captain looked at him with suspicion.

"Oh no, you won't. No way I let a boy like you fire this thing. Now show me what to do, and no tricks, now." Peter, feigning disappointment, nodded and stepped back to allow the captain to see more clearly.

"You light the match, and hold it against this piece of wadding, here. The powder will catch fire, and this spreads into the main body of the barrel. The rest of the powder will explode and propel this ball far out across the field. There will be lots of smoke, and a lot of noise. That means it's worked."

The captain nodded gravely. "Understood. Men, prepare yourselves!" He looked around, and Peter hurriedly stepped back. He began to walk towards the horses, hoping nobody would notice what he was doing. Luck seemed to be on his side now.

"Three! Two! One! Here we go ..."

The captain's voice faded into the distance as Peter broke into a sprint. He must get to the horses before ...

The force of the explosion hit Peter between his shoulder blades. He was knocked forward and stumbled on the grass, throwing his hands forward to catch himself. And then, in the smoke and the chaos, he clawed his way upright and ran for the horses. He dashed for the captain's horse, tore its lead from the hand of a dazed slave, and began to ride furiously through the choking clouds of smoke and debris towards the forest.

The horse responded powerfully to his urgings, leaping over low hedges and streams and galloping towards the green mass of trees on the horizon. Freedom! But Peter's heart sank as he heard the one sound he had dreaded, the sound he had hoped never to hear: the sound of other horses behind him. He was being pursued.

It was difficult to think about any strategy when he was so focused on guiding the horse to safety and staying upright in the saddle. His only plan was speed. The horse responded to his urging and pressed on towards the safety of the trees. It was a fine horse—a thoroughbred, he thought vaguely, a horse that would be a champion back in England, but he could not shake off his pursuers. He dared not look backward, as he might lose his balance, but kept pressing the horse for speed, more speed.

Minutes seemed like hours as his horse galloped towards the treeline, its nostrils flaring. He was nearly there! Maybe he could lose his pursuers in the trees ... Peter could see that there was a gap ahead, perhaps leading to a trail. The trees raced to meet him, and parted to allow him to enter their sanctuary. He guided the horse in the right direction, hoping it would not take fright at the mass of trees. And behind him, he could still hear the relentless beating of hooves. He had not been able to shake them off.

Peter reined in the horse, leading it off the trail and into the trees. He stroked his animal and spoke softly to it, dismounting. Peter stood in silence, waiting for his pursuers, hoping they would hear neither his own heart racing, nor the horse's heavy breathing.

Two figures passed by him slowly, clearly on the watch for him. Peter watched as one pointed and murmured to the other. They both dismounted and approached on foot. His heart pounding more than it had even during the explosion, Peter hurriedly searched around him for anything he could use as a weapon. There were no swords mounted on the horse's saddle and no good rocks lying anywhere about.

Peter looked up, aware that it had gone very quiet. And then, to his astonishment, he saw two slaves before him.

"Lord Peter," said the first, his head bowed low, "I believe we can help you keep safe from pursuit."

"I—what?" Incredulous, Peter kept a hand on his

horse's saddle, ready to flee at a moment's notice.

"We must go deeper into the forest," said the second slave. "They are sure to send out search parties. We must keep to the trees—tracks can be followed."

"I am Philip," said the first slave, sensing Peter's hesitation. "This is Andrew. We only need press on a bit longer, for the guards fear the woods. But we must go quickly."

"Come, let us go," said Andrew, and Peter nodded his assent. For what other choice did he have by now?

The trio remounted and headed into the forest. Peter could not help but notice that the slaves were leading him. They seemed to know where they were going.

Within the castle the Lords of Aedyn were huddled together in a conference, trying to make some sense of the reports that had reached them and the curious evidence of their own eyes. The cannon had exploded, igniting a nearby bag of gunpowder. Shards of clay and the explosive force of the cannon had seriously injured five guards, burning one of them almost beyond recognition, and that worthless captain of the guards had been killed instantly. It was, thought the Wolf, a grim day indeed.

He looked sharply at the man who stood trembling

before him. A grimmer day than most for him, he thought.

"Your fault again, Anaximander," he said without emotion. "You have failed as usual—failed miserably and completely. And now, before you die, answer me this one thing: Where is the traitor Peter, and when can I expect to have the pleasure of hanging him?"

Anaximaner cringed before the lords. He knew they would not be pleased with what he had to say, but his fate would be all the worse if he concealed it.

"There is no sign of the fair stranger. Nor is there any sign of the two slaves assisting in the … test."

The Leopard leapt from his throne with a snarl.

"Are you telling us that they have escaped? Three of them?"

Anaximander very much hoped that the earth would open up and swallow him. As it did nothing of the sort, he only nodded and continued.

"And three of the horses are missing as well. It looks as if the renegades seized the animals and made for the forest."

To this there was no response: the lords were silent. And then Anaximander saw that the Wolf's knuckles were white as he gripped the arms of his throne. He raised a hand to summon the guards, and the Lord Chamberlain was dragged, shrieking, from the Hall.

Without missing a beat, the Jackal turned to the others. "And what of this cannon? Do we conclude that it malfunctioned accidentally? Or that the traitor deliberately designed it to explode?"

"We saw it ourselves," the Leopard reminded him. "The captain fired the cannon, not the fair stranger. I suggest"—and here he began to look very proud indeed—"that we make more of these cannons and see if we can get them working properly. We have nothing to lose by doing so."

The Wolf nodded. "Very well. We may need these weapons soon if we are to face a threat from the forest."

Deep in the forest preparations were being made for the Great Remembrance. The seats in the garden were gradually being filled, although it was obvious that the garden had been intended to hold a much larger crowd. Many were absent. But the faithful few were gathered— Lukas and his band of men, dressed in their characteristic green, Alyce and Helen, and those who had not been conscripted to slave for the lords inside the castle. There was excitement in the air and rumors surged through the crowd. This year would be different!

Julia was led to a seat behind the stone chair where she
waited as the others took their places. She was dressed in
a radiant white robe. Alyce had helped Julia get dressed,
combing her hair until it flashed like gold in the early
evening sun. And now she waited to be called forward.

As the disk of the sun finally slipped from view
silence fell over the assembly. A great eagle flew down
from the heights of one of the surrounding trees, its majestic wings beating the air as it descended. It landed on
the ground in front of the great, empty throne at the
center of the garden. A few moments later, Gaius, also
dressed in white, mounted the throne. He looked out
over the gathered crowd and spoke.

"Friends, I am the keeper of our memories. You
all know that tonight is a special night. It is not like any
other night of the year. For this is the night of the Great
Remembrance, when we call to mind how we came out
of the doomed land of Khemia to this fair land of Aedyn!
The dark Lords of Aedyn have forbidden us to speak of
this, but truth can never be silenced! We must never forget the true story of the great exodus from Khemia. You
must learn this story by heart. Write it on your mind
and engrave it on your hearts! And remember well: the
story has not yet ended. It will not end until the Lord of
Hosts himself returns and redeems us."

Then he closed his eyes, and began to speak in a
voice that Julia had never heard before—a voice that

seemed not quite his own. It was a voice full of memory, a voice full of pain. The monk held within him five centuries of tears and anguish, she remembered.

"This night is like no other night," Gaius was saying. "For tonight we remember how the Lord of Hosts brought us all out of Khemia. He snatched us from the jaws of destruction and brought us to this rich and pleasant land. We remember with thanks his servant Marcus, who faithfully led us to this land."

Around her, Julia noticed that everyone was passing round morsels of some kind of food. Those who had plenty shared with those who had none. Alyce slipped across to where Julia was sitting and pressed something into her hands. Julia examined it cautiously. It appeared to be dried fish of some sort.

"On this night, we eat salted fish. Why do we eat salted fish on this night of the year, and on no other night? To remember that the Lord of Hosts brought us here across the great salt sea, to this good and fertile land. When we eat this fish, we remember what our Lord has done and look forward to what he will do. Brothers and sisters, let us eat, let us remember, and let us hope! One day the Lord will return! We live in hope!"

There was silence in the garden for a moment, broken only by the sounds of munching. Julia, who didn't like fish but figured this was no time to be picky, placed the morsel in her mouth and tried to swallow it quickly.

After each person had eaten, Gaius resumed his speech.

"Friends, we must never forget who we really are! We are the ones whom the Lord brought across the sea. We are the ones to whom he gave this fair land. We are the ones with whom he entered into a covenant, pledging to be faithful to us just as we were faithful to him—forever. Forever!"

Gaius looked around him. The tone of his voice changed again as he began to speak of how things had gone wrong—the great Question of Aedyn, Julia remembered.

"But there were those who wanted to be kings themselves. They wanted to rule, not to serve. They wanted power, not responsibility. We were betrayed, and we are now all slaves of the dark Lords of Aedyn. Their power comes from weapons, not from justice. This is not the way things were meant to be! We are faceless and nameless to these dark Lords. Yet—" and here a note of quiet gentleness came into his voice—"each of us is known by name to the Lord of Hosts. And nothing the dark lords can do will change this!"

Grunts, applause, and shouts echoed around the garden. But Gaius had not yet finished.

"Every year—every year for five centuries—we have hoped for deliverance. We have gathered in this garden to remember the past and hope for the future. Here is the throne of the Lord! And here is the altar at which the Lord made his covenant with us! They all lie in ruins. Still the Lords of Aedyn rule, and still we are trampled under their feet. But one day our paradise will be restored, and we shall once more be free!"

The crowd roared its approval. They lived in hope, even if each year that passed saw that hope dwindle a little. And who could live without hope?

Gaius paused. Normally, at this point in the story, he would ask them to be patient and faithful, and wait in hope. But tonight his message would be different.

"My friends, we believe that the Lord who we seek will one day appear in this land—his land! We believe that he will return, overthrow tyrants and despots, and establish his own righteous rule. And tonight I have good news to be proclaimed throughout this island."

The faithful gathered there were very still, not quite daring, after all the long years, to believe what they were hearing. This was what they had waited generations to hear, and it was almost frightening to believe that the day might be upon them. Gaius's bright eyes scanned the audience, waiting for the right moment to deliver his message.

"Tonight is different! For the Lord of Hosts has sent his messenger to prepare his way in this land and in our hearts! You all know the great prophecy of the coming of the Fair Strangers, written in our sacred books. The coming of these strangers was to be a pledge that the

Lord himself had heard our cries and taken pity upon us. One of them will deliver us! What we have longed for will take place! The Lord will deliver his people from bondage!"

The crowd fell suddenly and completely silent as Gaius stepped down from the stone throne. He returned a moment later leading Julia, her white robe highlighting her long golden hair. As she stood before them Gaius bowed down before her, then turned to the people.

"The Deliverer is here!"

The crowd rose to its feet. Time stood still. And Julia, who had never been anyone of much importance, found herself all of a sudden very shy and very excited at the same time. Finally, Gaius spoke again.

"Let the word spread throughout this land. The Lord of Hosts is coming! The old sorrows will pass away. The Lord will make all things new! You all know what needs to be done. Let us prepare for the restoration of Aedyn!"

The cheers resounded throughout the gathering night, wafting even up towards the distant citadel. The days of the Lords of Aedyn were numbered.

CHAPTER

16

W hat's that noise?"

Deep within the forest Peter and the two slaves halted. Their horses whinnied, made nervous by the noises to the west. Andrew and Philip glanced at each other and nodded.

"It's coming from the garden. It's the night of the Great Remembrance."

Peter looked askance at them. "What remembrance?"

"We ought to go there at once," Philip said. "It is a gathering of those who trust in the Lord of Hosts. It is a time when we hear the great story of our past. The dark lords suppress all talk about the Lord of Hosts. They hope that this will make us forget about him. But we could no more forget him than we could forget our parents or"—he exchanged a significant look with Andrew—"our children."

Peter did not understand at all but saw no reason to argue. They rode slowly towards the garden, guided only by the newly risen moon as they went along the darkened trails in the forest.

It was not long after—in fact, only a few moments later—that they rode into the garden. Peter recognized it instantly from the night they had spent there—it felt like ages ago. But the place was no longer abandoned. A group of men in green milled about excitedly. And who was that old man who seemed to be the center of attention? Why had Philip and Andrew rushed to speak to him?

And who was that woman in white, sitting on the throne? She looked vaguely familiar. And then Peter stared with astonishment. What on earth was Julia doing on that throne?

Julia became dimly aware of movement on the edge of the garden. Three new people had arrived. Two were slaves, doubtless late for the ceremony, but the other was different, his hair much fairer than the raven locks that surrounded him. Peter!

She clasped her hand to her mouth. She had never thought to see him again. She had never *wanted* to see him again. He was her brother, but he had betrayed her ... hadn't he? Julia was rooted to the spot, frozen by indecision. Part of her wanted to rush and embrace her brother; the rest of her wanted to run away from him as quickly as possible. And so she turned her head away from her brother.

Peter stared at his sister, wanting to embrace her—an emotion he could not recall ever feeling before. Yet she showed no interest in him. Was it that she was afraid of him? Or that he had done something wrong? Surely she realized that he had tried to save her life! Like Julia he stood still, not knowing what to do.

For some moments all was still and silent. Then Gaius strode forward, took Julia by the hand, and led her toward her brother.

"I think there has been some misunderstanding between you," he said with his characteristic simplicity. Julia's eyes flashed angrily.

"I think it is rather more than a misunderstanding, Gaius. I would call it a betrayal."

Gaius nodded. "Ah," he said. "And so it might seem to one who did not fully understand what he had seen. Come. Let us sit together and talk awhile." He turned and gestured them toward the pond that still shone silver. Peter and Julia sat down beside him at the bank, trying very hard not to look at each other.

"Peter, why don't you begin?" Gaius asked gently. "Tell us what has happened these past two days."

Peter took a deep breath and then found that he

didn't really know where to begin. But, glancing out of the corner of his eye at Julia, he knew that he had to begin with her.

"I didn't know what to do," he said. "I thought they were men of reason. I thought they were"—he gulped—"scientific. And they told me I could be a prince." He glanced at Julia shyly. "The lords had told us we were condemned to death—something about treason, I think. I decided to make a deal with them. I told … I had already told them how to make gunpowder, and all they needed was something to fire it in." He paused and again glanced sideways at Julia, who was trying her very best to look as though she were ignoring him.

"I told them I would show them how to make a cannon if Julia was set free."

Julia's eyes flashed open. So she had misheard …

"They agreed. I was put under house arrest while I designed the cannon, but I designed it so that it would fail. I would be there at the testing, and hoped that I might be able to get away in the confusion of the explosion that I knew would occur. I knew I might not have been able to, but I was happy to take that risk."

Gaius nodded, encouraging him to continue.

"The captain of the guard insisted on firing the cannon. It was then that I realized I would be able to escape. I walked towards the horses and took my chance. I had left a bag of gunpowder open near the cannon.

The sparks from the explosion would have made that explode as well. Nobody could see anything because of the smoke and I was able to get away on a horse." Peter shrugged and started picking absentmindedly at the blades of grass around his knees.

"And now, Julia," said Gaius, ever so gently, "perhaps you might tell your brother how you experienced things."

Julia was not sure what to say. What she had learned in the last few moments had made her deeply ashamed. She ought to have trusted Peter. He got things wrong, but he had not let her down. There was a world of difference between failure and betrayal.

"We were in that Great Hall and we had just been condemned to die. Then I caught snatches of a conversation … I thought Peter was making a deal to save his own life. I had no idea that he was trying to save mine instead."

"What happened next?" the monk prompted.

"I was taken to a prison cell. They called it the Death Cage." She fell quiet for a moment, and then spoke quickly, staring her brother hard in the eye. "I was about to lose my life and I believed I had already lost my brother. I don't know which would have been worse. And then I remembered the Lord of Hosts. I called to him and he sent me rescue."

Tears pricked at Julia's eyes, and she too

developed a sudden interest in the grass. "I'm sorry," she mumbled, and then she picked up her head and looked at Peter. "I'm so, so sorry."

"Come now," said Gaius. "The time for tears and distrust is passed, and we have more important work ahead of us. Lukas!" He called over, and Lukas detached himself from his band of men and made his way over to the pond. He knelt beside Gaius, nodding his head in a brief greeting to Peter.

"The time to fight is upon us," said the monk. "But first there is the matter of the children."

"As soon as we fight, they'll die," said Lukas simply. Gaius nodded, agreeing.

"So we'll have to free them first!" said Peter, and Julia raised her head and smiled at him. "Which leaves us with just the small matter of finding where they're being held."

"Ah," said Lukas. "Now in that, I believe, I can be of some assistance. Geoffrey!" He called out, and one of his men hurried over. "We need information on the children. Tell Gaius of your scouting mission."

Geoffrey was a sturdy man, not yet forty, and his arms rippled with muscles. His face was stoic as he spoke.

"There is a building that nestles against the hillside below the castle. We had always assumed it to be a storehouse for grain—for all we know, it *was* a storehouse until we escaped and they took the children—but on our last patrol outside the forest we noticed that the guards outside it had been trebled. It is surrounded by high walls, so high that two grown men could not see over them if one stood on the other's shoulders. The only entrance is a gate set into the walls. We could never hope to break it," he said.

"And you're sure the children are being held there?" asked Julia.

"So much as we can be, my lady," said Geoffrey. "What other reason could they have to guard it with so many men?"

"And how do we get the children if we can't get through the door? Do we climb the walls?"

"I think not, fair one," said Lukas. "The children would never be able to follow us out—not silently. And we could not risk the notice of the guards."

"This would be a perfect time for a bit of your gunpowder," said Julia, and Peter gave a sound that was almost a laugh.

"Would you take us there?" he asked Lukas. "Maybe we'll see something ... maybe we'll find a way."

Lukas glanced at Gaius, who nodded his approval. He stood, holding out a hand to help Julia to her feet. "You'll have to keep up," he said. "You must move silently. And you must move swiftly."

They stood just below the brow of a wooded hill, looking at a building in the near distance. Peter shaded his
eyes, so that he could see better in the late morning sun.
They had been walking all night, but far from being exhausted Peter was eager—perhaps a little too eager, in
Julia's mind—to storm the prison.

"How far is it from here?" he asked, his eye keen
on the building.

"It is a half hour's walk, Lord Peter," replied
Lukas. "And we would not be seen for the first twenty
minutes, as we would be passing through the wood. But
once we are beyond the trees, the guards will be able
to see us. We would not be in danger, as there are too
many of us. But the guards inside the building would be
forewarned. The whole building would be tightly locked
down by the time we got there."

"And there is no way of approaching it without
being seen?" asked Julia.

"No, my lady. We would have to walk there by
night if we were to avoid being detected." He paused,
sensing their disappointment. "There are twelve of us.
There could be as many as twenty guards, and they all
have swords. We have nothing but wooden staffs. They
will have the advantage over us, and it is only a fool

who goes into battle without the advantage. Even if we did manage to take them by surprise, they would soon recover. I'm not sure that we can win this one. And remember, they may have orders to kill the children if the building is attacked."

Peter peered hard into the distance.

"There seems to be a stream leading from the wood to the compound. Do you think someone could crawl along its banks without being seen?"

Lukas took a few steps forward, examining the stream and its steep banks with the trained eye of a master woodsman. He nodded.

"The banks seem high enough — enough to hide someone if they stayed flat as they worked their way round. They could make it to the outside wall and report back on what they found."

Peter considered his options. It might work. They would have to find the source of that stream inside the wood, and see whether its banks were high enough to act as a cover. He sighed. His first major military operation was not going to be easy.

Julia heaved a massive sigh — a sigh that indicated she was done playing and ready to go to work. "Come on," she said. "We can't waste any more time considering this; we've got to act. We need to get those children back to their parents." She looked at Peter and he looked back at her, and both children broke into enormous grins as they thought the same thing at exactly the same time. "Come on," she said again, and held out her hand to him. He took it in his and they began walking out from between the trees, leaving Lukas and his men behind.

They heard them spluttering—heard their protestations and the hissed orders to stop, to come back into the safety of the trees, not to throw their lives away just to play at being heroes. And then, as they walked out of the woods and into the full sunlight, the orders stopped as Lukas and his band of men melted back into the safety of the forest.

Peter and Julia walked on together, hand in hand, until they were close upon the gate. So close they could have run to it ... but now the guards had seen them, and had drawn their swords. They looked at each other, their fair hair tousled by the breeze, clenched each other's hands, and screamed.

The guards sank to their knees, hands clamped tight over their ears as the screams reverberated through the air. And then, above the noise of the screams, one could hear a cracking—faint at first, and then louder. If the guards had been looking they would have seen a fissure in the wall, and they would have seen that fissure grow until the walls fell down in a great cloud of dust.

And when the dust cleared, the walls were gone and the children were free.

They were hopelessly bedraggled—all of them dirty and too thin, but they were safe. They walked slowly, as if in a daze, the younger ones clenching the hands of their older brothers and sisters. They didn't recognize the fair-haired strangers standing before them, but then Lukas and his men came out of the forest and the children broke into a run, laughing as they ran into their waiting arms.

CHAPTER

17

The Lords of Aedyn had gathered for a crisis meeting in the Great Hall. Only Solon, the new captain of the guards, stood before them. Anaximander was rotting in a cell, awaiting execution for his treasonous acts.

"We face a catastrophe unless we act decisively," the Leopard was saying, pacing the smooth tiled floors. His hands were clasped tightly behind his back as he spoke. "Both the fair strangers have escaped. Our Lord Chamberlain has proved … untrustworthy. And the hostage children have been set free by those wretched outlaws!"

"Yes," said the Wolf slowly. "Please, Captain, tell us how that sad event came to pass."

Solon, who had told himself he had nothing to

fear from the lords in his new position, began to tremble.

"It ... it was something not of this world, my lords," he said. "My men saw the fair strangers approach and called to them to halt, but they would not. They drew their swords, ready to kill, and then the strangers ..." He paused, coughed, and looked around. "They screamed."

"Screamed," the Wolf repeated. Solon nodded, swallowing hard.

"Screamed, my lord. Screamed so that it might have shaken the sun in the sky. The sound of it knocked in the door and burst all the windows, and ... and it shook the chains from the captives. My men were paralyzed, my lord—their ears still ring with the pain of it."

"And the children?" asked the Jackal. "What happened to the children?"

"They ran out the door," said Solon miserably. "They ran out of the door and into the forest with the fair strangers."

"Ah," said the Wolf, and Solon began to tremble all the more.

"We are most displeased," the Wolf continued. "And had we not heard a similar tale about such a terrible scream from a patrol a few days ago, your life would not be worth the breath it takes to speak your name. Do you understand?"

Solon nodded. He understood.

"You will ensure that the guards are fully mobilized and ready to repel any attack from these bandits. It may come at any time. And you will make sure that the slaves never hear this news of the children."

The Wolf waved his hand. The audience was clearly over. Solon bowed and left the Great Hall as quickly as decency allowed, thankful to still be alive.

The Wolf paced the room after his new captain had departed, admitting to himself that, for the first time in centuries, he was worried. He fingered the ebony amulet at his neck as he pondered the situation. His grip on power was slipping, and there was now a real threat of revolt from the slaves.

The Leopard, seeming to read his thoughts, spoke up in the silence. "Everything is falling to pieces around us," he said. "There is no one left to trust—and no one who can stand against this new power. We are doomed!"

The Wolf turned angrily on his heel and spat his reply. "We have triumphed in the past and we will triumph again! Let me hear no more of that talk!" The Leopard, who had lived five hundred years without fear, began to be afraid.

The Wolf turned away from the Leopard as he continued. "We must now turn our attention to preventing a revolt within the castle. We shall institute a policy of terror. By the time we have finished with them, any thought of rebellion will die in their hearts. Guards!"

Two armoured men entered the Great Hall, silently awaiting their orders. "Fetch Anaximander from
his cell. Tell him that he will be restored to our favor if
he will show the slaves the meaning of fear."

By suppertime the children had been delivered to the
safety of the garden, to shouts and tears of joy. After an
evening of feasting and a good night of rest, Gaius, Peter,
Julia, and Lukas gathered over breakfast to make plans
for the liberation of Aedyn. They sat at a large wooden
table, a series of maps laid out before them, while not
far away in the garden Alyce and Helen sat mobbed in a
crowd of children, all shrieking with laughter.

Gaius was deep in conversation with Lukas
about military strategy, discussing how best to assault
the castle. They now had twenty swords, captured from
the guards the previous day. For the first time, they
would be able to meet the forces of the Lords of Aedyn
in combat.

"Twenty swords," Lukas was saying. "A help, of
course, but we'll be fighting scores—perhaps hundreds
of men. We simply don't have the numbers to meet
them in full battle."

"No, we don't," Gaius agreed bluntly. "But perhaps

there is a way." He turned to Julia, who had been largely silent. "Not an hour's walk from here there is a cave—a cave guarded by a messenger of the Lord of Hosts himself. In that cave are a hundred bows and quivers of arrows." Lukas' eyes went wide.

"You never told me of this," he said, his voice accusing. Gaius shook his head.

"Perhaps, my son, when you have seen five hundred years you too will find that it is sometimes best to keep secrets." His eyes twinkled beneath his heavy brow. "These are the arrows Marcus brought with him from Khemia—the arrows that the lords did not destroy. They kept them hidden, but I have put my own protections on the hiding place. A messenger of the Lord of Hosts stands guard at the doorway. None but the Deliverer may enter and take what is hidden," he said. "And that day is upon us."

Lukas leaned forward, his eyes bright.

"With arrows we can attack from a distance," he said. "Distract the lords with an assault and send a group of men around to free the slaves still trapped inside. With a hundred bows, I'll have enough to arm all my men and more besides for those who join us from the castle." He could see only one problem. "Gaius, can you teach us how to use these bows?"

The monk shook his head. "In my time I was a scholar, not a warrior."

"Then they aren't really going to be all that much use to us, are they?"

And Peter's face broke into a grin, because even if he was rubbish at Orienteering and Wildnerness Survival there was one thing he could really do well. "I think I might be able to help you there," he said.

It was later that afternoon when he and Julia set out to find the hidden cave. The walk was neither long nor particularly arduous, and they passed the time in a companionable silence.

Following the eagle, who flew just ahead of them, they soon found themselves at the foot of a hill. As they looked more closely they noted that the bushes and scrub, although long overgrown, seemed too neatly ordered to have grown there naturally. At one point, a curtain of vines and creepers reached from the ground up to the top of the hill. Peter began to draw it aside, pushing his way through the thorns and barbs to reveal a cave. So well had it been concealed that nobody could have found it had he not known precisely where to look.

He was on the point of stepping into the cave, Julia close behind him, when a voice boomed into his hears. He looked wildly about but there was no one near ... and yet the voice still rang in his ears.

"Who dares to enter here?" it roared. Peter looked frantically back at Julia, who came forward and laid a reassuring hand on his arm.

"We are Julia and Peter, the Chosen Ones," she said. "We seek the treasure you guard to restore this land to the Lord of Hosts."

A breathless pause, and then—

"Enter," said the voice, and then fell silent.

They went inside the cave. It was dark, but that could only be expected, and saturated with an earthy smell—the sort of smell you get in a damp room that has not been aired for a long time. After only a few paces Peter found himself bumping up against some wooden boxes. They were too heavy for him to lift, but he was able to pry the top off the uppermost container. He gingerly reached inside with one hand, privately hoping that there wouldn't be spiders, and was soon rewarded by the feel of a leather case. More confident now, he used both hands to pull out the case, his heart pounding. Even in the darkness he could see that the case had a distinctive shape—the shape of a bow. And there were quivers and arrows as well, carefully hidden beneath a protective layer of cloth. He had found the cache of weapons.

Julia, doing the same at the opposite end of the cave, gave at little cry of joy at her discovery. Only one question remained—would the weapons work? Or had they become worthless after their long disuse? There was only one way to find out. Peter extracted a bow from its case, noting with approval that the strings had been removed from the bows before they had been concealed. He carefully restrung one of the bows and fitted the nock of an arrow to the bowstring, making sure the string was properly aligned with the fletching near the base of the arrow. He carefully took the stance his archery coach had told him was the best, distributing his body weight evenly.

He held the bow in his left hand, drawing the bowstring back with three fingers of his right hand, two fingers below the arrow and one above, until his hand touched his chin. He raised the weapon and aimed for the tree ahead. A moment later he released the arrow, and felt the bow recoil in his hands.

The arrow missed its target, overshooting by at least twenty paces. Peter broke into a grin. The bow was far more powerful than any he had ever in the Scouts! He reached for a second arrow, adjusting his aim to allow for the unexpected strength of the bow. This one sank deep into the center of the tree with a satisfying thud. Julia broke into applause.

"It's marvelous Peter—marvelous! Come, we have to get Lukas's men to help us carry them back to camp!" She grasped his hand and fairly dragged him back onto the path. At last—at last!—they were getting somewhere.

As the sun was sinking in the west, Lukas's band of outlaws returned to the forest camp leading twelve horses heavily laden with the weapons. Peter supervised the stringing of the bows and the assembling of sets of bows, quivers, and arrows, marveling anew at their pristine condition. More of the magic of this place, he thought.

Julia watched approvingly for some moments, pleased that her brother's talents had finally been put to good use. She was confident that they would defeat the army of Aedyn and take control of the castle. If only that would be the end of this matter! But she knew it was not.

Gaius sought her out that evening as the small group of outlaws was bedding down, exhausted and eager for the rest. The children were huddled together as Helen told them bedtime stories, all of the young ones eager for the day close at hand when they would be with their parents again. As the fires sank low, Gaius motioned to Julia and she joined him, perched on a log beside one of the fires. Together they watched the embers glow and crackle with heat.

Julia picked up some fallen leaves from the ground and rolled them in her hands. They were highly fragrant, with hints of lemon and cinnamon. A smile came to her face. Why were wonderful fragrances so healing? They seemed to lighten her mood and heighten her awareness of the natural splendor of the forest around her. Why, she wondered, did such evil exist in the midst of such beauty? What had gone wrong? It was the most beautiful place she had ever seen, but it had become home to violence and treachery. Was it that people were weak and foolish, and failed to recognize evil when it arose?

Or was it downright rebellion against the laws of nature, the deeper structures of the world?

"You remember the question I asked you," said Gaius softly. Julia nodded, her hands still turning over the leaves. The monk seemed to read her thoughts.

"How evil could happen here," she murmured. Gaius nodded, his gaze on the dying embers.

"I want you to keep that in mind in the coming days," he said. "As we fight to restore this land, remember what it can become." Julia nodded, unsure precisely what to say. She would watch and remember—but why this question? And why her?

CHAPTER

18

The next day dawned as beautiful as the one that preceded it. The rising sun bathed the castle in its soft, warm light. A gentle wind tugged at the flag of the Lords of Aedyn, high on the battlements of the citadel. And far away the same sun filtered through the leaves of the great forest of Aedyn, waking those who would do their best to tear down that flag and replace it with the emblem of the Lord of Hosts.

Peter woke early from a dreamless sleep. He swiped away a spider that had spent the night as an uninvited guest inside his blanket and sat up to stretch his arms. Today he would train his troops for battle!

Peter threw his blanket to one side and went to a nearby pool to wash his face. Afterwards, he sat by the edge of the clearing for some moments. This was where the training session would take place later. It was ideal. The archers would stand at the north end and shoot southwards. He stood there for some moments, the early morning sun flaring in his golden hair while the soft, cool wind disheveled it. He must tidy himself up before the training session, he decided. After all, he wanted to command the respect of his troops — just like his father, who never appeared before his men in a less than pristine state.

And command them he did, as many hours of sweat and hard work found him, at the end of the day, at the edge of the forest clearing watching fifty novices practicing their archery. It had been a difficult day, but Peter knew his archers had become as expert as he could hope. There would be one last volley before they broke for the evening meal.

"Draw! Aim! Release!"

The air filled with hissing as the arrows sped on their way, thudding into the ground at the far edge of the clearing. Their shooting was not perfect, but it would serve. It would cut enemy troops to pieces and destroy their morale. Especially if they were expecting to fight slaves armed only with their fists and wooden staffs.

"Stand down! Collect your arrows!"

The archers walked to the far edge of the clearing to retrieve their arrows, and returned them to their quivers. They stood milling around, exchanging stories of how they had come to the forest and anticipating the battle that would take place on the following day. Some drank from the pool of clear blue water at the north end of the clearing. It had been a long, hot day.

Two figures, radiant even in their dull forest garb, emerged from the forest. The chatter died away as Julia and Gaius entered the clearing. They had been observing the final volley.

Gaius raised his hands. "My friends, I am entrusted with the story of our people. I have told you its past. How the Lord of Hosts called us out of Khemia to this paradise. How this paradise was lost. And soon I will be able to tell the story of paradise regained! For tomorrow we shall again make history. We shall march on the citadel and overthrow the lords who have enslaved us all these centuries. Your children will tell this story to your grandchildren, and they will tell it for many generations to come!"

He smiled as the cheers resounded throughout the clearing. "And now—" he broke into his twinkling smile—"Now you must eat! Fruit and bread are to hand. And then you must rest, for at sunrise we fight!"

He had barely ceased speaking when the familiar aroma of fresh bread began to spread through the clearing.

Peter was enjoying a particularly succulent piece of rare and refreshing fruit when he noticed Julia coming towards him. He scooted over on the log so that she could sit down beside him. She looked serene here, he thought—more at peace with herself than she had ever looked back in England. But then, he realized with a start, he had never really paid a great deal of attention to her in England.

They were silent for a long moment as they sat together, enjoying the fresh night air and the excited sounds of the freed slaves all around them. And then Julia asked something that Peter would never have expected:

"What happens if we die here?"

He looked up at her, startled. "We won't die here."

"How do you know? We're going into battle tomorrow. And we both know what those lords are capable of."

"Yes …" Peter nodded, and then put on his brave-older-brother face. "I expect we'll be fine, Julia. Just fine. And once the battle's over we'll find a way to get home."

"How?"

"I don't know."

And there was silence again. Julia leaned her head on Peter's shoulder and sighed heavily. "Sometimes I miss home," she said. Peter nodded wordlessly. "I miss Grandmother and Grandfather and I miss Scamp and I miss clean sheets and warm blankets. And I miss Mother."

"I do too," said Peter.

They spent another moment like that, sitting together and watching the fire burn, and then Julia lifted her head up and smiled at Peter. It wasn't easy to be a hero, they silently agreed, but the time had come to grow up.

CHAPTER

19

The sun was high in the sky as it beat down on Aedyn. The lords were gathered in the Great Hall, which offered a view of the approach to the citadel from the forest. This was the field on which the Lords of Aedyn expected the battle to take place. They had planned their strategy with meticulous care, but their ultimate triumph depended on the rebel slaves making a mistake.

If the slaves approached the castle from the west, they would walk straight into an ambush. They could easily be surrounded and picked off one by one. It would be a massacre. If they came from the north, however, they would be in a much stronger position. Yet even then the guards would be able to defeat the rebel slaves. After all, they had no weapons. And most of the slaves were still trapped inside the castle and had no way of taking part in the battle.

Solon rushed into the Great Hall, not pausing even to knock. "They come!" he cried. "They've been sighted leaving the forest. I'm mobilizing the troops, and the Lord Chamberlain has locked the slaves in quarters. They won't cause any problems inside the citadel."

The Wolf looked out the window, trying to follow what was happening on the ground in front of him. But the slaves were too far away to be seen properly.

"From what direction do they approach?" he asked.

"It's a little early to say, my lord, but it looks as if they plan to attack from the west."

The Wolf smiled beneath his mask. "Ah," he said briefly. "And so they will die."

Solon bowed his head. "Yes, my lord."

The Wolf turned from the window, his mask somehow more hideous than Solon had ever seen it.

"I want no prisoners but the fair-haired traitors. I think" — he looked at the Jackal and the Leopard—"I think we will rather enjoy hanging them at the end of the day."

Solon bowed and went to give the orders.

Peter watched the groups of rebel slaves marching towards the castle, puzzled by Gaius's strategy. They were going to approach the castle from the west. Even from here he could see the castle's defenses, the guards in place exactly where they ought to be. Surely Gaius must realize that he was marching into a trap? But his protestations had fallen on deaf ears, and Gaius had merely looked at him in that amused and all-knowing way of his. Peter walked along with a growing sense of doom: the guards would ambush them from two sides, closing off any avenue of retreat.

But he had his instructions. He was to march his archers north, keeping just inside the forest as long as possible. He was then to approach the castle from the north, and wait for Julia's signal before firing. He marched on, sullen but determined.

Another guard entered the Great Hall and held a hurried consultation with the Lords.

"Solon sent me with news," he said, breathing heavily. "A second column approaches from the north. The main column is still coming at us from the west. What do you want us to do?" He waited as the Wolf turned from his station at the window.

"Deploy the reserve guard on the south side of the citadel. They can block the advance of this second group. Once we've wiped out the main column, we can turn our attention to them."

The guard hesitated, unsure of the procedure. Who was he to question a Lord of Aedyn? But this was too risky.

"My Lord, that means our entire guards corps will be deployed outside the castle. We'll be left with only a handful of guards inside."

"We are not expecting an attack from within, are we? We need our forces outside to make sure that none of these outlaws escapes alive." The guard nodded.

"Of course, my lord."

The two groups of rebel slaves were closing in on the citadel. The guards watched them restlessly, their swords at the ready. Surely they had nothing to fear from these runaway slaves. They had only a few stolen swords. Their doom would be swift.

Peter led his men forward, estimating range. The guards were in a defensive posture, waiting for them to attack so that they could hack them to death with their swords. He paused. They were in range, but best to be sure. They marched another twenty paces. They could see the guards ahead of them, their swords itching for action. He held up a hand for his men to halt, waiting for the signal from Julia.

And then, from the west, he heard a scream—not as loud as it might have been had he been standing close, but it would serve. He turned toward the men and yelled with all his might:

"Draw! Aim! Release!"

The air was thick with arrows, hurtling down mercilessly on the guards. Several fell dead; others looked around, desperately, trying to work out what was happening.

"Draw! Aim! Release!"

Another withering volley hissed through the air before falling to find their targets. The guards looked around, terrified. They broke ranks, retreating hastily and in disorder towards the castle. As they did so, a series of massive explosions rang out on the east side of the castle. Billows of acrid smoke enveloped the area.

The Jackal, looking down on the scene from the citadel, turned to the others, an expression of utter delight beneath his mask.

"The cannons worked!" he cried. "Even the noise they make will be enough to terrify those fools down there! And just wait until those cannonballs slice them to ribbons. They haven't a prayer." The Wolf joined him at the window, and as the smoke cleared the scene below told a different story.

The cannons had not killed countless rebels but had exploded, killing the teams of guards who were operating them. A troop of horsemen seemed to have come from nowhere, armed with swords to finish off the remaining guards. Slaves newly escaped from the castle were swarming everywhere, picking up swords form the hands of wounded and dead guards and using them to fight alongside their brothers. The lords' ambush had failed miserably.

And what was this? To the south, the guards sent to engage the second column were in total disarray. Some were lying dead on the ground and others were in full retreat, heading for the safety of the castle gates.

The Wolf leaned forward, unable to believe what he was seeing. Slaves were thronging inside the castle, shutting the gates and preventing the guards from getting back to safety. His retreating guards were trapped between the castle wall and the advancing rebels. He watched in horror as a volley of arrows shot upwards and descended on the hapless guards, who had nowhere to run for safety. Where did they get those weapons?

Suddenly there was a noise immediately outside the doors of the Hall. The three lords turned just as the doors crashed open, revealing the bodies of dead guards lying outside. The rebels who had killed them had views about the men inside the room.

It was, perhaps, the first time the Wolf had been taken aback in five long centuries. He gasped as slaves armed with swords approached them and backed them into a corner. They were trapped. They were doomed.

And then the rebels parted as a young, fair-haired woman entered the Hall. She was hardly recognizable as the emissary from Albion, but had a new look about her—a look that knew what it meant to be chosen. And it was in this look that the lords finally found fear.

But the Wolf was no coward, nor was he a fool, and only a fool would enter a battle unarmed. He touched his long fingers to the dagger concealed within his robes.

"So, little girl, you've come to take over the world."

Julia shook her head. "No. Only return it to those who will serve it best."

One of the rebels approached, his knuckles white around the hilt of his sword. But Julia put out a hand and touched his arm.

"No, Lukas," she said. "We show them mercy."

At that word the Wolf struck. No one saw the dagger fly out of his hand until it was too late.

Julia cried out as the dagger struck her cheek. A curtain of blood fell over her face and she crumpled to the floor.

Lukas was with her in an instant. The wound was not deep—that much he could see—although it would leave a mighty scar. Julia blinked up at him. She was in pain, but she was conscious. Lukas rose and stood eye-to-eye with the Wolf. He reached out and took hold of his mask, wrenching it away from his face.

The face exposed there was no longer human. The mouth and nose had grown out from the rest of the face into a snout and the lips curling up in a snarl revealed massive teeth. The eyes shone bright and yellow—and angry.

Lukas turned away from him to the Leopard. "You surrender?"

"I rather think we do," he stammered.

Peter was still outside the castle, organizing his men and dealing with all the thousands of details that come after a battle, when he noticed Helen and Alyce emerging from the forest. They were surrounded by a bevy of children who clung to their hands. Peter grinned and nodded a greeting to them as they approached the massive doors of the citadel, out of which the freed slaves were running.

Perhaps you can imagine the joy they felt at the reunion—the tears, the cries, the long embraces. Perhaps you can picture the jubilation of a child who has been too long without a parent. It was a sight to make the stars dance in the sky.

And Peter, who suddenly missed his mother so much he could hardly breathe, felt tears pricking at the corners of his eyes and turned away.

It was an hour later that Julia, her face pale and swathed in bandages, and Peter entered the Great Hall of Aedyn together to the cheers and applause of the faithful. After so many centuries, they had never expected this day to arrive. The old order was passing away, and the new would begin. Peter held up his hands for silence and waited for his sister to speak.

"We were called here by the Lord of Hosts to lead you from darkness into light," she said. "The former things have passed away. The Lords of Aedyn have been vanquished. Their power over you is broken. Bring in the masks!"

Those assembled stood on tiptoe as the three grotesque masks were brought in by three bearers, trying to see what was happening. Each of the masks of the hated Lords of Aedyn was placed on a wooden table before the throne. The crowd watched with bated breath as Julia held up each mask in turn.

"These masks were worn by weak, evil men. They wanted you to fear them and respect them. And you were fooled by this crude deception. You will never be taken in again! Watch!"

The masks were placed on the table. Lukas marched to the table, sword in hand. With three massive strikes, he destroyed each mask.

"And now ..."

The Jackal, the Leopard, and the Wolf, such as they were, entered the Hall at sword point. They stared straight ahead, oblivious to the gasps at their deformed faces. Peter went to them and removed the ebony amulets from around their necks.

"Your years are coming to an end," he said softly
—so softly that only they could hear. "You will die
alone, and you will die soon. Your power is broken." He
brought the amulets to Lukas, who, at a nod from Gaius,
forced the point of his sword through each one of them
in turn.

As the last amulet was broken under the sword,
Gaius spoke to the lords. "You will know the sting of
mortality," he said. "But not just yet, for mercy is stronger still. We send you not to death, but to exile. You will
return to Khemia, the land you left all those years ago,
and live out the remainder of your days."

The lords were escorted (none too gently) out
of the Hall. Peter and Julia were led to the old thrones,
and if you had heard the cheers you would have thought
that it was angels singing.

CHAPTER

20

The afternoon sun blazed down on Aedyn. A zephyr rustled a flag flying from the great citadel of the island, bearing the emblem of the Lord of Hosts. Crowds of people were milling round the castle, clearing away the debris of battle and exulting in their new freedom. Lukas had taken charge, ready to ensure a smooth path from oppression to peace.

Peter and Julia walked among the people, stopping to grasp hands and exchange stories with those gathered. And then Gaius found them and ushered them away.

"Come," he said. "There is little time."

And as he spoke the walls of the citadel melted away, and they were once more in the garden. The silver glow was stronger than ever.

Julia looked around in utter astonishment. Gone were the ruined walls, the overgrown paths, and the blocked fountain. The soft stone walls were covered with roses and flowering plants, whose heavy aroma perfumed the late afternoon air. The fountain was burbling, sending cool streams of pure, clear water into the air and cascading into the pond. The garden was serene, an oasis of coolness in the heat of the day. It was as if an army of gardeners had labored for weeks to restore it to its original beauty.

Julia wandered around the walled garden, admiring the flowers and their delectable fragrances. In another part of the garden she found some trees, whose beautiful broad green leaves seemed to exude sweet-smelling oils which hovered in the air. One tree was set apart from the rest, raised up and surrounded by a low stone wall. Its branches drooped low, laden with exotic ripe fruit. She returned to the center of the garden and the great throne where Gaius and Peter were waiting.

"Well, fair one?" the monk asked. "Have you solved our great question?"

"I think so," she murmured. "It's all about power, isn't it—loving power more than people."

"Nothing's that simple," scoffed Peter, but Gaius raised a hand to silence him.

"Truth is found most often in simplicity," he said. "You have done well, my children. You have set this land free from its oppressors, and so it will remain for many years."

"Not forever?" asked Julia.

"No. Not so long as the dark power that created those amulets exits." Gaius shook his head, and then looked up, beyond the children and beyond the garden—beyond Aedyn itself. "But one day, a redeemer will come. One who will be of the house of Marcus, but greater still. One who will defeat the dark forces of evil and death. We can only resist them, but he can break the true source of their power and banish their presence. The Anointed One will come. We are his heralds, and we prepare his way. His hour has not yet come."

As he spoke the sun began to set, and a cold breeze blew throughout the garden. "It is time," said Gaius. "Tell no one of the things you have seen here, but remember … always remember."

His voice faded, and the garden seemed to glow more brightly than ever until the silver overwhelmed their sight. And when it faded, Peter and Julia found themselves no longer in Aedyn.

"My goodness!" It was their grandmother, come to find them in the garden. "Both out of your beds after midnight—after midnight! You'll catch your death of cold! Come inside the house, and let's warm you up and get you safely into bed. Your father's coming tomorrow with something special to tell you, and I don't want him to find you still abed!"

Peter and Julia exchanged glances, and then, silently agreeing that it was best not to say too much, nestled under their grandmother's arms and went up into the house.

We want to hear from you. Please send your comments about this book to us in care of zreview@zondervan.com. Thank you.

ZONDERVAN.com/
AUTHORTRACKER
follow your favorite authors